THE SECOND SECRET

ALAN LEE

Copyright © 2017 Alan Janney

First Edition
Printed in USA

Cover by Inspired Cover Designs

Paperback ISBN: 9780998316574

Sparkle Press

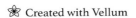 Created with Vellum

For my children
Jackson
Chase
and Rima Grace

1

Kristin Payne and I spent the evening at River and Rail, a precocious bistro in south Roanoke with polished wooden tables and reverent servers. We sat near the front window and heroically ordered the chef's special. Our waiter was a severe man who whispered, and he brought us cocktails and deviled eggs.

"The problem, Mack," Kristin told me, "is that I'm an athletic girl."

"Ah, poor thing."

"I'm not fat."

"I noticed," I said.

"When you're strong, when you play softball in college, when you maintain an active workout schedule into your thirties, it doesn't matter how much you diet. I'm not fitting this ass into size eights."

"So you're a size ten," I noted helpfully.

"You know Gina Carano?"

"Heavens yes."

"That's me," said Kristin and she took a drink of her elusive pear, a house specialty.

Kristin was something of a blast from the past. We'd spent a

memorable seven minutes between classes inside a science department supply closet, sophomore year of college, and then tried to meet
up socially for a while but it never happened. My son's sitter had
ambushed me with this blind date but seeing Kristin again had not
been an unpleasant surprise. Her dark hair was cut in a ragged bob,
she wore no jewelry, and her white knit top had a plunging neckline.
Of which I took no notice, Lancelot that I was.

"Whatever number, you are wearing the hell out of those jeans," I
said, a momentary lapse of chivalry.

"The denim is stretchy and the heels help. But thank you."

"Can you punch as hard as Gina?"

"Doubtful. But I bet I'm close on the front squat."

"As an act of charity, I'll pay for your meal anyway."

She said, "Roxanne tells me you're a private investigator. I didn't
know that was a real thing."

"Fell backwards into it. I taught a couple years, and I miss that."

"Taught?"

"High school English," I said.

"You're enormous."

I shrugged. Modestly so.

She said, "You can't teach English. You should be the football
coach."

"I've received a few calls about being an assistant. Coordinating
the defense. I might."

She snapped her fingers.

"I remember, now. You're the teacher who shot his co-worker. I
heard about this…a couple years ago?"

Our food came and she ordered another elusive pear.

"Right? That was you?" she asked.

"Shot him to pieces, yes."

"I forget why."

"He voted for Bernie Sanders."

She coughed and nearly spit out her drink.

Mackenzie August, master of wit.

"That's funny," she said.

"I know."

"But seriously."

"Man I shot had kidnapped my son. My opinion, I let him off easy."

"Didn't the guy die on the spot? Front lawn of the school?"

"Exactly."

"Have you shot anyone else since?" she asked.

"A gentleman never tells."

"So you're like Kinsey Millhone."

"Yes but she has better legs. Perhaps I'm more like Mike Hammer."

Kristin had an aggressive sensuality about her. She was physical. Fit. Proud of it. She sucked the barbecue sauce off her finger and she knew she looked good doing so.

I asked, "What do you do? Roxanne didn't tell me."

"Assistant professor of cultural psychology at Roanoke College."

"So you're Dr. Payne now."

"Has a great ring to it, right? And I coach field hockey."

"If you're into psychology, are you diagnosing me?"

She grinned, with a mischievous twist.

"Sizing you up? Analyzing your problems?"

"I don't have any of those," I politely corrected her.

"Tonight I'm simply a gal on a date. All I've diagnosed is that you have broad shoulders, thick biceps, and great hair."

"My hair is short," I said. "And unpretentious."

"But it's all there and you use product," she said. "It hasn't changed drastically since college. Do you remember that afternoon in the supply closet?"

"Doesn't ring a bell."

"Yes it does. I sent you away with a smile on your face. I even remember your cologne. And the smell of bleach."

"That's a hard one to forget. Though it's been over ten years."

She shrugged and finished her second drink. "You were the starting middle linebacker. Lotta girls pined after you. And some boys are worth remembering."

"You're not wrong."

"You married what's-her-name, right? What happened?"

"Krystal," I said. "She died unexpectedly after moving to New York. We never married. I went to California and joined the police force so I could legally kill everyone."

"Wow, once a linebacker, always a linebacker, huh?"

"I like to think I've changed."

She gave a lazy smile.

"Not too much, I hope. I liked the boy in the supply closet."

"You've stayed single."

She tilted her head back and forth in partial agreement. "Meh. I've called off two engagements so far. Men are pigs. And so am I, possibly."

"You are suggesting a degree in psychology does not an expert make?" I asked.

"I do not practice what I preach."

"Physician, heal thyself."

"Fancy quote for hired muscle," she said. "And here I was toning down my affectation."

"I wish your restraint rubbed off on our waiter."

"Going to ask me out again?" she asked.

"Sure."

"Buy me another drink and take me home, Mack."

I did. She lived in Salem, near her place of work. She had the top floor of an old white house with faded wooden slats. Academia didn't pay, apparently. I parked out front and put the car in drive but let the motor run.

"Come inside?" she asked. "Want to see how far you get?"

Yes. I did want to see. A lot. Like most men I knew, I was a human being. Built with wants and needs. And she was a woman, healthy, full of vitality and promise. I was nearly breathless with the idea. But I'd been asked this question before and I'd accepted. Many times. Not once — not once — had it ended well.

"Mack? Walk me up. I'm three drinks in. Three drinks could mean third base," she said and she stumbled through her R's.

"You're a professor of psychology. How would you diagnose your potty mouth?"

"You get to take the professor's clothes off." She grinned and covered her mouth. "How about that?

"I can't," I said, ignoring thousands of years of evolutionary biology which were screaming at me. "I'm late to relieve my sitter already."

It was a lie. I couldn't think past the thundering in my ears.

"Don't you get lonely?" she asked.

"I do."

"God, I get so lonely. Are you lonely right now? At this point in your life?"

"Kinda."

"Come on, Mack. Let's go be lonely together. I got ideas about stuff we can do to forget the lonely. Fun stuff."

"I can't. But let's go out again," I said.

What the hell was wrong with me.

She said fun stuff. I liked fun stuff.

Get out of the car, Mack. Turn off the damn engine.

"So you're not coming?"

I didn't answer.

"What're you afraid of?" she said, barely making the transition from "What" to "you."

"Being untrue."

"You havfa girlfriend?"

"Being untrue to myself."

"Ugh. Fine," she said.

I got out to get her door but she kicked it open and walked purposefully to her staircase.

"See you," I said.

"If you're lucky."

2

It was a beautiful late March. Temperatures in the mid-fifties, the skies were clear and business was booming.

Except I didn't want to do any of it. I needed a day off from photographing romantic trysts, searching for missing teenage runaways, and foiling insurance fraud. So I did what all trusty and industrious private detectives do in their downtime; I searched for new grill recipes online and practiced drawing my gun from the holster, Wild West style.

Fortunately for me, and also for the client, I was sitting at my desk when the stairs creaked. Someone knocked softly on the door and entered.

A blonde. She wore a white blouse with an exaggerated collar and one of those skirts which was already too short and then had a professional slit running halfway up the side. Red heels. No hose.

She was perhaps the prettiest person I'd ever seen in real life.

"Hello, Ronnie," I said.

"I am in need of a professional private detective," said Veronica Summers. "Are you accepting clients?"

"I'm your man."

The gravid statement hovered and the air became hot and electric. She inspected me. I watched her inspecting me. Both of us flushed a little. I almost flinched each time our eyes connected.

She said, "Mackenzie. I'm serious. This is a professional call."

"Then you should put on an overcoat."

"But how would you look at my legs?"

"I have a degree in criminal investigation. I'll find a way," I said. "Close the door behind you."

"If you're accepting clients and you think we can work together, I'll go fetch him."

"Fetch who?"

"The client," she said. "My father."

"Oh."

"You were hoping for a damsel in distress? One wearing a tiny skirt?"

"More like a damsel in distress with a bag of money."

"He's loaded," she said.

"And his skirt?"

Ronnie smiled.

The room brightened.

My heart nearly stopped.

"Take his money, Mackenzie. And I'll keep wearing the skirt."

"Bring him in."

She went to fetch him and I wiped sweaty palms on my pants. Get it together, Mackenzie. You're a grown man. With a gun.

Ronnie and I had recent history. Though I hadn't seen her in three months, I pondered her daily. If I was stranded on a deserted island and got to take one thing she might be it.

No. Wait.

I had a son. I'd take him.

But if I could take *two*…

She returned with her father, a genteel silver fox. Perfect part in his cobalt hair, a faint tan, blue suit worn unbuttoned, white cuffs peeking from his sleeves, shiny deck shoes. He smelled of money and power and the awareness of it. The family resemblance was strong. He entered and Ronnie closed the door.

I stood.

"Not much of an office," he said, waving offhand.

"Perhaps you were looking for a dentist?"

"I'm looking for a man who gets things done."

"Such men do not spend time on decorations."

He nodded. "Fair enough."

We shook hands.

"Calvin Summers."

"Mackenzie August. Please sit," I said.

He sat. So did Ronnie and she crossed her legs. I pointedly did not watch, which was even more difficult than turning down Kristin Payne. I believe she enjoyed my discomfort.

"My attorney tells me you're good," he said.

"Ms. Summers is your attorney?"

"She is." He indicated her with his chin. "You've worked with her before?"

I glanced at Ronnie. She was rigid, anxious, and she gave her head a slight shake.

"Not much. She referred some work my way. And those went well."

"I need you to find someone," he said.

"I can do that."

"But I don't know who. I know that doesn't make sense yet." He leaned back in the chair and picked invisible lint from his pressed slacks. "I run a small organization and someone inside is disloyal to me. I want the fucker found out."

"How many persons do you employ?"

He waffled his hand, which gleamed with a college ring. Looked like Virginia Tech. "It depends. Call it...fifty, in various capacities. Only ten of whom directly answer to me. For example, I own a restaurant. The restaurant has approximately twenty employees, but I only communicate with the manager. You see."

"I see."

"Can you do this?"

"I can. It will involve snooping into your affairs, however."

"Hell, everyone else does. You can be discreet?"

"Can, must, and will."

Ronnie placed a hand on his arm to get his attention, but he shrugged her off.

I hoped she was appreciating my exhaustive efforts at professionalism. She was on edge about this encounter, which was why thus far I hadn't mentioned his obtrusive Confederate flag belt buckle. Or his complete disregard for her.

"My business is sensitive, Mr. August. What assurances do I have you won't report what you find?"

"None, I suppose. We could shake on it."

"Shake on it," he repeated. With displeasure.

Ronnie shifted in her chair.

"Pinky swear?" I offered.

No response.

I said, "I do not share my client's information. With anyone. If, after discovery of your unsavory and sordid secrets, I decide I'd rather not work with you then I will simply quit. But that won't happen."

"Veronica tells me you used to be a detective in Los Angeles?"

I nodded.

"Any leftover Boy Scout sentiment?" he asked.

"Boy Scouts do not last two days in Los Angeles. What business are you in, Mr. Summers?"

"I own commercial investments. Some of it under the table."

"Local?" I asked.

"All investments are within forty miles. I live at the lake."

"How do you know one of your employees is disloyal?"

"Because two weeks ago I was released from Ashland, after spending an unpleasant six months there."

"Ashland," I said. "The white-collar prison in Kentucky."

Ronnie kept her gaze fixed on her legal pad.

He said, "Yes. I reached a plea deal with the fucking US attorney. I forget the details. Something like a fine and twelve months for tax evasion, released after six. A cushy establishment, but I did not enjoy it. Nor did I enjoy my embarrassment."

"And one of your employees tipped off the feds," I said.

"Almost certainly."

Ronnie spoke up. "So you understand, Mr. August, why neither he nor I, his attorney, would want details of the situation circulating."

"Of course."

"Your discretion is paramount."

"Of course," I said again.

"Will you be working with anyone else on this case?" she asked, making notes.

"Possibly."

"Who?"

"Whomever I choose. You'll need to trust my judgement or find a different investigator," I said.

Calvin Summers shot his daughter an irked glance of death. "Grown-ups are handling this. Take notes, and that's it. Understand?"

She ignored him. "If you use someone else I'd like his or her name, Mr. August."

"You'll get no one's name, I'm afraid."

"You're not married," she said.

"No."

"Dating?"

"Sure," I said. "More or less."

Her pen stopped. "You are? Who?"

"Does it matter?"

She said, "She'll need to be vetted. Conflict of interests."

"Hey," Calvin said. "So he's seeing someone. The fuck do we care? Close your mouth."

"When would you like me to start?" I asked either of them.

"Yesterday. I want this guy burned. How busy are you at the moment?"

"Two open cases, other than yours. I have time. Where can I get the names and addresses of your employees?"

"My attorney will provide them."

"Would you prefer your employees not know that the enterprise is being investigated?" I asked.

"If possible, yes."

Ronnie asked, "What is your hourly rate?"

I told her.

"Good hell." Mr. Summers chuckled to himself. "Everyone believes they've got a medical degree these days."

"What's her name?" Ronnie asked.

"The woman I'm dating?"

"I'm simply being cautious."

Ahh jealousy. I luxuriated in it.

Mr. Summers glared at her again. "The hell's the matter with you? I don't care who he fucks. Jesus, got'damn lawyers."

"I don't mind," I said. "Her name is Hester Prynne."

Ronnie wrote down the name. Frowned at it. Then turned her sparkling, impish eyes back to me. She knew the name, knew the character, got the joke. Her father didn't.

She tried to hide her smile with businesslike frustration but she failed.

Calvin stood. "When you visit my idiot fucking lawyer's office, her receptionist will cut you a check for the retainer. We have a deal? You find the guy who alerted the authorities?"

I did *not* like him calling his daughter an idiot fucking lawyer. He'd barely looked at her during our meeting. Hadn't admitted the family ties. I took a moment to debate the merits of throwing him around the room.

"We have a deal," I said.

Why?

Because I hated him.

Because I wanted to be near Ronnie.

Because I wanted to remove him from his money.

Because I wanted to "find the guy who alerted the authorities" and shake his hand.

Very unprofessional. It went against my code of conduct.

What fools we mortals be.

"I'll start tomorrow," I said.

He nodded and left without another word.

On the way out, Ronnie stopped and her hand alighted on the doorknob. "Mackenzie. Now you know my second secret. My father is a convicted felon with an ongoing criminal enterprise. And I'm an accomplice."

I nodded and asked, "Are you a willing accomplice?"

"The jury will say I am, if they find out."

"What would you say?"

She shrugged, which looked good. "I do the work. So..."

"Do you do it willingly?"

She didn't respond for a moment. I watched her face, and missed being able to look into those blue eyes more often. A tear spilled down her cheek. "I miss you, Mackenzie."

She closed the door.

3

My trusty Honda had been treated unfairly and maliciously by a pack of evildoers last fall. Rendered unrecognizable out of sheer spite and perhaps out of revenge for me costing the evildoers millions of dollars. Sheriff Stackhouse arranged for some policy akin to worker's compensation to coordinate with my insurance to provide a new trusty Honda. An Accord with less than ten thousand miles. I felt like the top one percent.

I parked my gleaming ride off Stoutamire Drive and knocked on the flimsy screen door of a rented home, belonging to a man who had zero dollars allocated to home and yard maintenance. An old Nerf basketball hoop stood luridly askew in the knee-high brown grass.

Jake White answered the third knock. He looked swollen and exhausted. Wore ancient board shorts and a white T-shirt. "What, dude," he said and he glanced at a watch on his wrist, a watch which did not exist. "What time is it..."

"Nine in the morning and I'm afraid all the worms are gone. I'm Investigator August, working on behalf of Brad Thompson."

"Who? Damn, it's early."

"Brad Thompson is an attorney," I reminded him helpfully. "You're the primary witness at a jury trial scheduled next month."

"So?"

"So you claim Timmy Diaz shot your friend, man named Rodney."

"Fuck yeah, Timmy shot Rodney. So? Jesus, you're a big fucker."

"Me or Jesus?"

"What?" He blinked. Stupidly.

"I bet I'm bigger than him. Jews were short two thousand years ago."

"What? Do you care if I sit down?"

I entered. He sat on a couch which looked as though it'd spent two months on the curb and he closed his eyes.

"Run me through the events of that night one more time," I said. "Please."

"Why."

"I said please."

"Timmy shot Rodney. Blaow, blaow. Right in the fucking hip. Now Timmy goes to jail. Because Timmy is a prick."

I opened a file and pretended to read from it. "You're friends with Rodney."

"Yeah."

"Timmy and Rodney were arguing."

"Yeah."

"Timmy The Prick pulled a gun."

"Yeah."

"Police still can't find Timmy's gun. But all three of you agree it was the revolver which belonged to Timmy's father. Right?"

"Right."

"A Ruger Blackhawk," I offered.

"Whatever."

"Timmy's father said it was a Ruger Blackhawk. He has the paperwork."

"Cool, shit, whatever, man."

I pressed on, despite his daunting intellect. "You said Timmy shot Rodney because of revenge. Timmy claims it was self-defense."

"Right. Revenge. Not self-defense. Timmy lies. Remember? Timmy's a prick."

I said, "Timmy said it was self-defense."

"Timmy's bullshitting. He's a bullshitter, you know?"

"If it was self-defense, which Timmy says it was, I bet Timmy would have cocked the gun first," I said. "Know what I mean? Pulled the hammer back, like 'You guys better back up or I'll shoot.' Right?"

"I guess."

"Did Timmy cock the hammer first?"

"No way man."

"Timmy just started shooting?"

"Just started shooting," Jake said.

"So no warning? Just bang bang?"

"Exactly. You got it, man."

"How many shots?" I asked.

"Two."

"First one missed. That's what Rodney says."

"Right. Two shots. First one missed. Timmy can't hit shit."

I pretended to write things down in my file. "Two shots. And Timmy cocked the hammer first? As a warning?"

"No, man, what'd I just fucking say? He didn't warn. Just started yanking the got'damn trigger."

"But Timmy cocked the hammer before the second shot?" I offered. "To threaten you?"

"No. No Timmy didn't ever cock no hammer. No warning. No threatening."

"Timmy said he did."

"Who the fuck are you, again?"

"I work with Brad Thompson Law and he—"

"I don't care. Timmy's lying. Never cocked the damn gun. Because it wasn't in self-defense. Get it? Now get out."

I snapped the file closed. "Thank you for your time, Mr. White."

The screen door slammed weakly behind me and I got back into my sparkly new Honda spaceship. After I'd driven two blocks away, Brad Thompson raised up from his reclined position in the backseat.

"Hiding in the back is a bit dramatic."

"I know." Brad grinned. "But I always wanted to do it." Brad was a good-looking guy from Detroit, blessed with a natural scowl. He was still in his twenties, young to be operating his own law firm. "What'd you find out?"

"Jake White is lying. He has no idea how a single-action revolver works. Claims Timmy never cocked the gun, which is impossible with the Ruger Blackhawk."

"Huh?"

"Trust me. That gun has to be cocked. Jake says he never did," I said. "Which is false."

"So Jake is lying. To help his buddy Rodney".

"Yes."

"His testimony won't hold up if I press him about the gun."

"Precisely. Under the conditions he set forth, that gun wouldn't fire. Hammer has to be pulled back first."

"I think I might demonstrate that in front of the jury. It'll be gorgeous," Brad said. "Discredit the witness."

"Agreed."

"You're the best, Mack."

"I know this."

"Are you working on anything else?"

"Ronnie Summers sent something interesting my way," I said.

"Oh yeah?" he said. We paused for a moment of silence, during which we each quietly marveled at how absolutely uncompromisingly attractive Ronnie was. This was necessary whenever her name came up. Lesser men did this audibly with sexist and objectifying comments, but Brad had class and morals and a cute wife.

I broke our reverie. "What do you know about her father?"

"Not much. Rich. Busted for tax evasion, I think? Couldn't get him on the big stuff, so both sides settled."

"Big stuff?" I asked.

"I only know rumors. Money laundering, maybe drugs. Are you and Ronnie an item?"

"She's engaged to a man in Washington."

"Ah."

"Ah."

"I didn't know," he said.

"Neither did I. There's much I don't know. Like, who was the prosecutor on Calvin Summer's case?"

"I'll find out."

"Many thanks," I said.

I PICKED my son up from Roxanne's house at five. Some days I got him at eleven in the morning, some days as late as eight. He called me, "Daaa," with great enthusiasm and graced me with open arms.

That still hadn't gotten old. And it never would.

"Good day?"

"Very. He's always good," Roxanne replied. Brown hair, glasses, sweatshirt, no makeup. "Kristin said your date went well."

"It did. Your stock has risen, in my eyes."

"Kristin said she threw herself at you but you refused."

"The things girls share with one another, in my educated opinion, are weird."

She frowned and cocked her hip to the side. "Did you not notice her abs?"

"I noticed. And admired."

"I don't get you, Mack. I'm trying to help."

"My hot water heater has a leak. Could you fix that?"

"Are you dating someone else?" she asked.

"Not technically."

"But..."

"But."

"Will you ask Kristin out again?"

"Almost certainly. You'd like a videotape of the encounter, I surmise?"

"No." She laughed. Because I'm clever. "A juicy summary will suffice."

I drove home through the quaint Grandin neighborhood. Today was the first day of spring. Daffodils bloomed in full glory and the dogwoods were budding. Not lemonade and lawn mower weather yet but we were close.

A woman bedecked neck to ankle in athletic wear was stretching on the sidewalk in front of our house. I'd seen her before about this time; she competed with two other local joggers, circuiting into view over and over and over, hoping to be seen by my roommate, guy named Manny. I was straight and even I could see Manny was worth the effort. I pulled into our driveway and did my best not to leer.

Unfortunately for the Spandex-ed and nubile athlete, Manny was on the back deck grilling and still wore his blue marshal shirt. He saluted me with his Michelob Ultra and gave Kix a high five.

"Hola. What's for dinner?"

"You see the chicken strips," he said.

"Sí."

"You see the steak strips."

"Sí."

"You see the peppers and onions?"

"I do."

"But you cannot figure out what is for dinner?" he asked.

"Would have saved a lot of time, you said fajitas."

"I teach you to think, Mack, instead of giving you rote answers."

"Much appreciated. But my white privilege would prefer not to think."

"How you people made it across the Atlantic is a mystery."

I said, "There's a girl on the front sidewalk, hoping you'll notice her."

"Qué? Who?"

"Short brown hair. Spandex."

"Shorts? Green stripe?" he asked.

I carried Kix in the crook of my left arm and he was dangerously close to falling asleep, a disaster of nuclear proportions at this time of the evening. "Pants, not shorts. Pink stripe."

"No, gracias. She drives a Prius."

"What if it'd been a green stripe?" I asked.

"No, gracias. That one has cats."

"You're a hard guy to please, Manny."

"No, amigo, I'm simply looking for a girl with no faults."

We ate dinner in the living room at the front of the house with the television on. Windows open, pleasant spring cross breeze. We watched the NCAA tournament while Kix nursed his bananas, bits of chicken, and juice, and Manny bemoaned the dearth of Hispanic basketball players.

Timothy August, my father, came in late from a dinner date still wearing his blue sports jacket. I'd quit inquiring after his dates because they often involved Sheriff Stackhouse, an arrangement I found especially jarring because, if permanent, I would have a mild Oedipus complex. Local magazines had run out of reasons to put her on the cover.

He poured a vodka soda and joined us. Kix soon nodded off on the couch beside me. There we stayed until midnight, enjoying the soft sound of squeaking sneakers, the cheering of March Madness crowds, and the unspoken familial bonhomie.

4

Ronnie's office was off Salem Avenue in a renovated brick building. Easy parking, great view of the railroad, second story. Unlike other offices in her building, hers did not have an opaque glass door. It was heavy wood reinforced with metal and had three redundant locks. Impressive alarm system too. Daunting door but charming interior, cream walls, polished hardwood floors, and a circulating scent of expensive perfume.

I entered, a man in full possession of himself. On a mission. Incapable of being sidetracked by pretty lawyers with brilliant smiles. Her receptionist, identified as Natasha Gordon by the nameplate, looked up from her expansive desk. She was pretty, in a young, brown-haired, hardworking, paralegal sort of way. A bluetooth headset was in her ear. "Welcome to Summers Law Firm, how can I help you?"

"That's quite a desk," I said.

"Thank you."

"Have you tried landing model airplanes on it?"

She blinked. "I'm sorry? Beg your pardon?"

"You know, pretend like it's an aircraft carrier."

The reception area had four points of egress — the door I'd walked through, a bathroom, a conference room, and Ronnie's inner office, which *did* have an opaque glass window, a sure sign of a competent lawyer.

Ronnie threw open that door and appeared.

Enter the goddess.

She said, "Only you would walk through and make such atypical observations about her desk."

"Poor Natasha has too much territory to cover, like she's playing center field."

"Hello Mackenzie."

"Hello Ronnie."

Natasha looked concerned.

"Let's chat." Ronnie beckoned me into her office and closed the door after. I sat in one of the two client chairs. She sat in the other and crossed her legs.

"Is that a skirt?" I asked. "Or a napkin?"

"I knew you were coming by today. I debated wearing a shirt only."

"I have time, if you'd like to change."

She asked, "How have you been?"

"My cholesterol inched up a few points. So not great."

"And your perfect angel baby, Kix?"

"He misses you," I said.

"Not nearly as much as I miss him. I promise you. Is he walking and talking yet?"

"He's a hero. Heroes don't age."

She smiled and shook her head. Her blonde hair was up in a messy bun, the kind with chopsticks thrust through. The strands framing her face swayed slightly, an effect I deemed purposeful and effective.

"I'd forgotten how fascinating your answers are."

"Why me, Ronnie?"

She took a deep breath, which looked good on her, and released it. "I've asked myself that too."

"Calvin Summers could hire any number of guys to roust the informant."

"I think the simplest explanation is, I want to be near you." Her neck and cheeks colored with a pink patina.

"Why."

"Basic mating instincts."

My pulse thundered.

I mastered myself. A man in full possession.

"Are you still engaged?" I asked.

"Yes."

"Ah-hah."

"Ah-hah?"

"Esoteric investigator jargon. I just uncovered your lurid background."

"You knew I was engaged," she said. "It's not a romantic arrangement. He fools around, I know. So..."

"So..."

"There's a couch." She indicated the leather chaise lounge couch behind me with an innocuous tilt of her head. "Right there. Begging for use."

"You're seducing me."

Her right leg was draped over her left knee, and it pumped up and down with excitement. "Attempting to seduce you. Thus far, I've been embarrassingly inept at it."

"If I let you then you'd no longer want to be near me, to borrow your phrase."

"What evidence leads you to this verdict?"

"Because I'd no longer be worth it," I said.

"That's not true."

"The regard with which I view myself would drop. And that would be the beginning of the end."

"Because I'm willing to be attained, does that make me less worthy?" she asked.

I didn't respond.

She visibly flinched. "Oh..."

"I make zero judgements, other than of myself. I don't hold you to my standards."

"But...I think, maybe you should."

The red high-heeled shoe slipped off her foot and her bouncing toe moved in dangerous proximity to my pant leg. If we made contact, all hope was lost.

I asked, "Can I get the locations of your father's holdings?"

"Yes."

"And names and contact information of his employees."

"Yes."

Without breaking eye contact, she slid a small stack of papers off her glass-topped desk and laid it on my lap. Attached to the top was a check. With an impressive number written in elegant calligraphy.

"What's her name?" she asked.

"The girl I'm dating?"

"The lesser and inferior girl you're dating, yes."

"Kristin."

"Kristin? Just Kristin?"

"Just Kristin."

"I'll find out who she is," Ronnie said.

"And?"

"And she'll be in danger." She smiled. Curvy lips. Perfect teeth. Sharp white canines.

"Ah, but your hired muscle would refuse that morbid assignment. Because he's dating her."

"I didn't say I'd hire you to hurt Kristin. I'll do it myself."

"Wow," I said.

"I'm the jealous type."

"And yet you confess your fiancé runs around?"

"He's not worth the jealousy."

Her toe grazed my leg.

The air was thick and hot, like inhaling steam.

I stood.

"I'm fleeing," I said.

"Why."

"You win this round. I'm a bit overwhelmed. Prone to poor decisions."

"Hah!" She stood and beat me to her door. Blocked it with her body. "The indomitable and stoic Mackenzie August admits to human frailty. You want me."

"I've never hidden that."

"I know. But. My spring just brightened by an entire color palette, hearing you admit it."

"You have issues, Counselor Summers," I said.

"Say it. You want me. I want to watch your lips move."

"What an unusual word fetish you have."

"Only for those words issued from your mouth."

We were close. She smelled of perfume and coffee and breath mints.

"Ronnie."

"Yes Mackenzie."

"Move away from the door."

"Yes Mackenzie."

She did but her hand stayed on the knob.

"I'm working on it," she said.

"On what?"

"On being the kind of girl you want to be with."

"I do want to be with you," I said.

"I know. But I don't want to be a guilty pleasure. To borrow your phrase, I want to be worth it. If I find a way to extract myself from my father's illegal enterprise, I will."

"Your second secret doesn't disqualify you."

"Oh?"

"It's your first," I said.

Some of the energy went out of her eyes. "I know. The fiancé. I know. And my third secret?"

"I tremble at the thought."

She opened the door and said, "Yes. Goodbye, Mackenzie. I hope you'll see me again. Soon."

5

Calvin Summers owned three trailer parks, six upscale Smith Mountain Lake vacation rental homes, an Italian restaurant, two convenience stores, and a small dairy farm. All located inside Franklin County, the rural county directly south of Roanoke. An impressive list. Nothing on here struck me as sleazy or illegal. But I was willing to bet that wasn't all he owned. Call it a hunch.

My first stop was at his property manager's office in Westlake. Freshly built structure — it still had the hollow feeling of being inadequately furnished. Mr. Stokes's office had nothing on the walls yet. He stood from his faux-wooden desk and shook my hand briskly, like an industrious man with much to do before quitting time. He was bald and wore those glasses that clicked together at the bridge.

"Good to have your boss back?" I asked.

"Sure, sure." He shrugged and leaned back in his swivel chair. "Though truth be told, there's an awful lot of freedom while he's gone."

"That's precisely the reason I chose a career with no supervisors."

"Sure, I get that, sure. Don't get me wrong. Fine guy, fair boss. But you understand."

"I understand."

"What do you do, Mr. August?"

"Commercial expansion consultant. Mr. Summers would like to considerably expand his holdings, and he asked me to be involved. First things first, I'm getting the lay of the land."

Mr. Stokes nodded and pondered the implications of increased responsibility.

I said, "I assume you know why he spent six months in prison."

"Tax evasion. I didn't ask a lot of questions. Doesn't change my opinion of Mr. Summers."

"You don't handle the finances?"

"A little. I collect checks from renters. I submit the expenses for home repair. Things like that."

"To whom do you submit checks and receipts?"

"Bradshaw. Tom Bradshaw, Mr. Summers's accountant. Fine man, has an office not far from Ms. Summer's. His attorney."

"His attorney and his daughter," I said without thinking as I wrote down the name Tom Bradshaw. He'd been left off the list.

"You met Ms. Summers? Holy hell, is she a treat to look at."

"She is exquisite," I agreed. "What properties do you oversee?"

"Rental homes, convenience stores, and Little Venice."

"Little Venice, the Italian restaurant."

"Yes sir. I ran into Ms. Summers once at her father's house. She wore this little yellow bikini, you know? Walking around like it was nothing. I tell you what. Thought about that day ever since."

"Keep you warm all winter, eh, Mr. Stokes?"

"By God, it did."

I smiled. Better than punching him in his teeth.

"Who manages the trailer parks?" I asked.

"The mobile home lots each have a superintendent. Don't recall their names. Wayne Cross oversees them all. Deals with water, sewer, disputes, things like that."

Wayne Cross was on my list. The superintendents were not.

"In your professional opinion, Mr. Stokes, is the enterprise run well?"

"The enterprise, sir?"

"Mr. Summer's business. Run efficiently? Effectively?"

He nodded. "Oh, sure, sure. Tight as a drum."

"You're satisfied with your salary? You'd assume Mr. Cross is too?"

He smiled modestly. "My salary is about what I'd get from other property management offices. Got no complaints. Can't speak for Mr. Cross, though."

"Do you know him well?"

"Not well, no sir. He's one of them Franklin County boys, Southern to the bone. Big guy. Loud truck. Know the type?"

"I know the type."

"Keeps the mobile home renters in line, such a big fellow, you understand me."

I asked, "Do you ever have trouble with the convenience stores? Or the restaurant?"

"No sir, not a thing. Stores get burglarized now and then but that's common."

"Big moneymakers?"

"Again, I'm not the expert on that. I don't balance the expense and revenue books. But I had to guess, I'd wager the restaurant breaks even and the convenience stores are a gold mine. Just my opinion."

"What do you know about his dairy farm?"

He made a big zero with his thumb and fingers. "Zip. Don't know a thing."

Thusly we continued. How often were the rental homes occupied? Were there any regular renters who stayed long periods of time? How many different managers had the restaurant employed? Had any employees recently quit that he knew of? And so forth. Finally, near the end, I caught him off guard.

"If I wanted to steal from Mr. Summers, how would I do it?"

His swivel chair righted itself, its occupant sitting up straight. "Steal?"

"Mr. Summers wants to grow his business. I'm looking for weak areas. How would I steal from him?"

"Well, now, I don't know that you could."

"Sure I can. There's always a way. How would I?"

"Got no idea."

"Let's get creative."

"I suppose...hm, maybe you could rob his tenants?"

I shook my head. "I don't want to steal from *them*. I want to steal from Calvin Summers. And for him to never know about it. How would one of his employees do that?"

"Has one of his employees done that?"

"Not to my knowledge."

"I reckon the restaurant manager could skim food? Short the cash register? Same with the convenience stores."

"Let's say that happened. And you found out about it. What would you do?" I asked.

"I'd report them."

"To Mr. Summers."

"Yessir."

"You've never had to?"

"No sir, I haven't. And it's a mighty weird question."

"Have you ever fired anyone?" I asked.

"Not me, no. I helped evict a few mobile home renters. I'm sure Little Venice has released employees."

"Could you collect a rental check from a vacation home at the lake and not report it?" I asked. "Cash it yourself?"

"I would never."

"I know. But could you?"

"I suppose. But the rental calendar is monitored by both his accountant and Ms. Summers. Or I guess I should say, her receptionist. They'd know."

Stokes's desk had no photographs of family. No souvenirs from fancy vacations. A spartan workplace. "Do you live nearby?" I asked.

"Burnt Chimney. Ten-minute drive."

"How long do you plan to work for Mr. Summers?"

"Long as he'll have me. I enjoy it. Pays the bills."

"Thank you, Mr. Stokes. You've been very helpful."

~

TWO OF THE trailer parks were near Rocky Mount. I visited both, the first of which was off Highway 40, named Ferrum's Fields. As far as trailer parks went, Ferrum's Fields looked upper-middle class. The majority of yards were clean and mowed, no rusted cars out front, no hanging doors. No decrepit dog cages, no junk piles. These were double-wides with decks and screen porches.

The second park, however... Hard to look at. Like a third-world country. Half the units were set on cinder blocks and suffered from sunken or busted floors. Pit bulls, feral in appearance, held on thin chains. Thirty-year-old antennas, broken trucks, hanging shutters, elderly couples staring vacantly from plastic lawn chairs. Piles of empty beer cans and cigarette butts. The scent of sewage.

My gut clenched.

The name of the park was Happy Hills.

When was the last time Calvin Summers had been here?

I supposed it wasn't his responsibility to enforce quality of life standards or a work ethic, but certainly part of this disaster belonged to him. This looked like every bad stereotype of deep Appalachia. Like *Deliverance*.

I circled the lot three times, feeling heavier in my soul each circuit.

A man stepped out of a trailer near the exit. He wore boots, boxer shorts, and a gray tank. Desperate was his need for a razor, deodorant, and a toothbrush.

He flagged me down and I lowered the window.

"Help you?" he said. "Lookin' for something?"

"Wayne Cross. He around?"

"What'cha want with Wayne."

I took a guess. "You're the superintendent of this fine establishment."

He didn't answer.

"How often does Wayne come by Happy Hills?"

"The hell kinda question is that," he said.

"Ahh… numerical? Or you could respond with a date from the calendar?"

He didn't answer.

"Does the name Calvin Summers mean anything to you?"

"Means nothing to me and neither do you."

"I'm grieved to hear it. How quickly can we get Wayne here?"

"You a cop?"

"I am not. I'm here on behalf of the owner, Mr. Summers."

"Probably time you moved on."

"Not going to invite me in?" I asked.

"Invite you into where?"

"Your home. You know, hospitality?"

"No I don't know." He smacked the flat of his hand against the roof of my spaceship. "Get on. Folks here don't like strangers."

I dropped my car out of drive and into park. "I have a couple water bottles in the back. Want one?"

"You got about half a minute, 'fore I call the dogs."

I got out of the car. Stepped into the dirt. He retreated a pace. I moved in such a way that he could see the pistol clipped to my belt, small of my back.

"I'm here because the owner asked me to be. He wants to make improvements." I retrieved my wallet and put three twenties into his hand. "And you could make my life a lot easier."

"Big fucker, ain't ya. What do you do?"

"I help businesses expand. Right now I'm looking at yours. I'd be grateful for suggestions."

"Suggestions? Shit. Burn it all down. Get all new mobile units."

"That's an option. But. These are homes to the people who live here."

He looked quizzically at the bills in his hand. "Wayne know about this?"

"Not yet. Talking to him next. Anything you say to me, he'll never hear."

"Wayne's fine. Hates this fuckin' place but he's fine."

"You don't know the name Summers?" I asked.

"I know it. Met him once. Fancy shoes, fancy hair, bullshit like that."

"That's him. What do you do here?"

He nodded to the park, which would buzz with flies once the temperature rose. "Keep all them people occupied. Keep 'em dumb until they die."

"What do you mean?"

"You know. Keep their cable on. Bring 'em cigarettes. Their shine. Their pills. Toilet paper. They don't move much. Then one day soon they'll fuckin' die and I'll get someone take their spot."

"How do they pay for their rent and for your services?"

"Government checks. Sign 'em over to me. Or Wayne."

I said, "So this is essentially a rest home."

From hell.

He nodded. "Last stop before the grave."

"Everyone here is elderly?"

"Most. Or sick or stupid or something."

"How do you fill their prescriptions?"

He grinned. Not a good look. "Said I get them pills. Didn't say no prescriptions."

"So they come here. And never leave."

"Some of 'em, yep."

"And you take the checks issued by the government, and handle all their needs."

"That's about it."

I did some quick math in my head.

If the average Medicaid and Medicare check was a thousand bucks, and I guessed maybe a hundred residents lived here, then he was taking in one hundred thousand dollars a month. No idea what he was spending; not much, based on the evidence. Ballpark — seventy-five percent of the income. That left twenty-five thousand dollars for the superintendent, Wayne, and Mr. Summers to split. Each month.

Extremely profitable side business.

Except almost none of Happy Hills was legal.

I bet Calvin's name wasn't officially attached to any of it. Or maybe he had built-in protection.

"Police ever give you trouble?" I asked.

"Nah. Matter fact, they send folks our way often as not. I keep troublemakers quiet."

"With medication and liquor."

"This here's Franklin County." He spit out a plug of tobacco. I hadn't realized he was dipping. Must be swallowing the juice. "We use shine."

"Moonshine. Produced locally."

"Yep."

I said, "And you live here, rent free, and keep a modest percent of the profits."

"You got it."

"And somehow you fall asleep at night."

"It's a living. These people don't gotta stay here."

"What about a health inspector?" I asked.

"Hell, everybody's got a price."

~

I USED the drive-thru at McDonalds in Rocky Mount. Parked, sat with my eyes closed, and tried not to think about what I'd just seen.

And also I drank a chocolate shake.

I knew places like Happy Hills existed. A large percentage of rest homes and mental health facilities were essentially cleaner versions of Happy Hills. Done legally and with more powerful drugs.

But still.

Part of what churned my stomach was Scott. That was his name. Scott who? Just Scott. A man almost as unhealthy as the park he oversaw. Dead-eyed Scott. Hell, everyone's got a price.

Ronnie had never been to Happy Hills. I'd seen her working at the Rescue Mission; she had a heart. A soul. She would never approve of Scott or his methods or of Happy Hills. She'd quit first.

I hoped.

6

Manny and I got breakfast at Scrambled, a downtown eatery. Despite the morning chill, we sat at an outside table because we were intrepid. I ordered the famous vanilla French toast, because I was a glutton. He ordered the eggs and sausage, because he forsook carbs and liked to feel superior.

The waiter brought our food and went back inside.

"The waiter," Manny said. "Name's Seth."

"So he told us."

"Hombre's a wanted man. Fraud and missing child support."

"Yikes. Seth struck me as responsible."

"Ay caramba."

"He's on your case load, I deduce."

Manny nodded around his coffee. "Sí."

"Going to bust him?"

"No. I like Scrambled. Need to maintain the relationship."

"But you're a US Marshal," I said.

"Not a good one."

"Yes you are."

"Yes I am," he agreed. "But I'm ahead of the others. Jefe thinks I work too hard."

"It's that Hispanic industriousness."

"So," he said. "Your girlfriend's papí is an ex-con."

"Ronnie and I are not dating. But yes."

"Someone snitched on him."

"Someone snitched on him," I agreed. "Calvin believes it's an employee. So far he hasn't mentioned family. Or past business associates. Or enemies."

"And you, Señor Detective, will find the person."

"I will."

"But you won't tell Calvin Summers," he said. "Even though that's what he's paying you to do."

"Probably not. Hard to tell, at this stage."

"Seems like a bad way to do business, amigo."

"I don't care," I said. "He belittles Ronnie. Abuses her in multiple ways, I'd guess. I hate him."

"Ese coño."

"Assuming coño means something bad, I agree."

"Any leads?"

"Just getting started. I need to visit his dairy farm next."

Manny's eyebrows rose a half inch. "Tienes un trabajo loco. Need backup at the dairy farm? Could be cows."

"I'll manage."

BILL OSBORNE MET me for lunch at Tucos Taqueira, a new margarita bar near the jail. We ordered tacos and looked longingly at the liquor shelf, but abstained. Because we were stalwarts. Bill was a US attorney operating out of the Roanoke office; he wore a white button-up which needed replacing, sleeves rolled, and frayed at the seams. He had a kind of nervous twitch in his shoulders.

"Brad Thompson called me," Bill said. "Said I should meet you but didn't tell me what for."

"I need a drinking buddy," I said.

"Yeah, he told me you're quirky."

"He said quirky?"

"You know Brad. Too classy to call you a weird motherfucker. Also, he told me about that pistol thing. The revolver was single-action, or whatever, and that will discredit the witness. Pretty slick."

I held up my hands — all in a day's work. "Any officer could have done that. It's you attorneys who don't know anything."

"That's what my wife says. You were a police officer?" he asked and he glanced at his phone. He struck me as the kinda guy who did that a lot. Power player, full of his own importance — the world would end if he ignored it too long.

"Detective in Los Angeles."

"Now a private investigator in Virginia?"

"Yep," I said.

"Maybe your career's going the wrong direction."

"You're a terrible drinking buddy."

He laughed. I'm a riot. Our food came and we tucked in.

"Are you the PI made the news last year? Helped with the Sergeant Sanders thing?"

"That was me," I said.

"You were there? At the shootout?"

"I was there."

"Jesus," he said and he twitched his shoulders. "Awful night, right? I heard about some of it. The parts that didn't make the papers. You the guy got stabbed?"

"Under my left arm. KA-BAR. I don't recommend it. Putting on a shirt is still an adventure."

"I knew Sanders. Shame about that. Good guy." He checked his phone.

"Perhaps we've digressed," I said. "I've been hired by Calvin Summers."

He coughed around his taco. "Bullshit."

I did my best to appear sheepish. Which wasn't easy.

"He really hired you?"

I nodded.

"Calvin wants revenge, I bet. He wants to know what tipped us off," Bill said.

"Who."

"Yeah, who. That's what I meant. Can't believe you took that asshole's money."

"Mainly because I thought he should be parted with as much of it as possible," I said.

"Got that right."

"I'll figure it out. Shouldn't take me long. But I'm unsure what to do afterwards."

Bill twitched his shoulders. "What do you mean?"

"I don't plan on telling him."

"Then what the hell are you doing?"

"I'm not sure yet. He angered me," I said.

"That's it?"

"That's the easiest version."

"Sure, I get that. He's a dick. But, Mack, some advice. He's not a man you want to be enemies with."

"That isn't a problem which concerns me."

Bill checked his phone.

"Okay. Well. I can't really help you," he said.

"I know this. I also know he's into more than tax evasion. Professional instincts. What I want to know is, why such a light sentence?"

"Wasn't so light. Hefty fine, two years in prison, reduced to six months. But yeah could've been worse. Hell, you know how it is. All I do are plea deals."

"He settled quickly," I said.

"Too quickly. But listen. I should say this again." He learned forward conspiratorially. "He's not a simple selfish old man with dubious business ventures. Calvin Summers is connected. Powerful. Rich. Don't piss him off. I mean it."

"I quake."

"You don't scare easily, huh. Don't say you weren't warned."

"What else is he into?" I asked.

"Don't know. We didn't do a thorough investigation. Got him on the taxes and quickly processed it. Our office is understaffed. You going to share with me everything you uncover?"

"I don't betray clients. At least not to that extent."

"What'd he do to piss you off?"

"Long story. Does he have any priors?" I asked.

"Nope. Squeaky clean."

"And your informant arrived out of the blue?"

"The informant was referred to me by a Roanoke City commonwealth attorney, who said the informant arrived out of thin air. Calvin's a big deal but we run in different circles. I'd never heard of him. His daughter, on the other hand..." He grinned. They all did that.

"You've met Ronnie."

"Of course, she was the dependent's attorney. But everyone knows Ronnie. Very sharp. Good at her job. She's also what I see at night when I close my eyes."

"She has a good reputation?"

"Shit yeah. She's sort of a general practitioner of law. I've seen her in both the state and federal courts. Handles criminal stuff. Employment and corporate too. Only works with the wealthy. Sort of like a concierge service. Rich people love Ronnie. Can't blame her for picking the clients who pay more."

"Any chance she ratted out her old man?"

"No. None." He glanced at his phone and during the interval he realized he'd said too much. He'd eliminated one of my suspects. His shoulders twitched.

So it wasn't Ronnie. On top of that, she'd seen the evidence and still didn't know who it was. That narrowed my search.

...somehow.

I was super good at my job.

"What evidence did the informant present," I asked, "which convinced you to pursue Calvin Summers?"

He shook his head. "Won't tell you that. But it was black and white. A no-doubter."

"Would your informant have testified?"

"Probably. But we didn't get that far. Ronnie pressed for a plea deal immediately."

"She can be convincing," I said.

"Politely phrased. I'd leave my wife for Ronnie."

"Ah, but then you wouldn't be worth her."

"What?"

"Nothing."

7

Timothy August, the patriarch of our crew, watched Kix that evening while Manny and I graced the local karate dojo. After-hours it transformed into a mixed martial arts gym. Local fighters practicing for Titans of the Cage. Sweat and blood and testosterone in the air, mats on the floor. That kind of thing.

We worked the heavy bags, the speed bags, the jump rope, and took one of the smaller rings to work with our gloves. Some of the older guys acted as coaches, growling instructions like, "Close the distance, *then* punch," and, "With your knuckles, jackass, not your fingers." They yelled at me more than at Manny.

Manny was more of a natural fighter. He grew up doing it; his arms thundered like pistons, his legs uncoiled like springs. If boxing was soccer, he'd be a quick striker and me the thicker goalie. He resembled Cristiano Ronaldo, which helped my brilliant analogy — he'd even had his teeth done in his early twenties, giving him further arresting powers. He wore a black Armani T-shirt and it galled me to be outmatched by such a twit. I hoped my Nike outfit was ashamed of itself.

At the end we toweled off and took water. One of the spectators clapped from his metal chair and said, "You two motherfuckers look like a *CHiPs* rerun."

Our spectator was a man named Big Will, a local gangster. Short guy, thick muscles, heavy beard, shaved head. I'd run into him a couple times last year, chasing down his employer. His sweatshirt had one of those sweat rings around the neck.

Manny asked, "Don't know CHiPs. Is that an insult?"

"Not for you," I said.

"You want me to shoot him?"

"Can try," Big Will said. "Lot more of us in here than you two honkies."

Our conversation was being monitored with interest by men sitting in adjacent metal chairs and possibly by onlookers behind us. Friends of Big Will's. And probably of mine, once they got to know me.

Manny noted, "He called me a honky."

Big Will inclined his head toward Manny. "Hey Ponch, thanks for letting my brother slide. Big of you."

Manny waved it off. "Figured he didn't pay taxes so hombre doesn't deserve my services."

For my benefit, Big Will explained, "My brother's a wanted negro. Couple bullshit charges. Ponch here tracked him down. Like he's a fucking drug dog."

"Ah," I said. "Manny the drug dog."

"Named Ponch?" Manny asked.

"It's an old television show."

"Ponch and me, we cut a deal," Big Will said.

"Financial?"

Manny shook his head. "Big Will, now he owes me. I like getting these negroes in debt."

"I'm not sure you're allowed to call them that," I said. "You know. Proprietary discretion."

"How's the arm, white man?" Big Will asked me.

"Silva stabbed me in the left latissimi dorsi, not the arm. My fastball remains in the upper nineties. Sweet of you to ask."

"Coulda been worse, honky. A lot worse. Shoulda been. Don't know why Marcus went easy on you."

"I have excellent teeth. Rigorous dental regimen. Floss every night. That's probably it," I said.

Big Will didn't seem amused, which was odd. "You're lucky Marcus got pull, you get it? You don't know the half of it. Not the fucking half."

One of Big Will's compatriots, a giant fellow, all mass and no definition, said, "Hey marshal. You're that marshal."

Manny nodded. "Sí. That one."

The giant said, "You're the marshal took down Chilly."

"Chilly the Kid." Manny laughed quietly and drank more water. "Sí. I liked Chilly the Kid. That was a good fight."

"Taking down Chilly ain't easy," Big Will said.

Manny said, "Depends. Didn't seem so hard."

"Heard you holstered your gun, Marshal," the giant said. "Heard you fought him with your fists."

Manny shrugged. "I needed a workout."

"You fucking fought Chilly?" Big Will asked. "The hell's wrong with you. Next time just shoot the nigger in his foot. Chilly the Kid's been hired muscle for Marcus before. He'll kill you next time, Marshal. I've seen Chilly break a man's teeth with a backhand."

"Didn't say he hit lightly. Just say he lost."

"Crazy Mexican."

Manny said, "Earlier you said Marcus got pull, amigo. The Mafioso?"

Big Will nodded. A slow and meaningful motion. "With the fucking Mafioso. Up in DC. District Kings."

"Marcus Morgan works with the District Kings?" I asked. Even lowly Mackenzie August, humble and handsome private detective, had heard of them. They were the brains behind the money behind the muscle.

"Marcus works with everyone. Especially the Mafioso. The District guys, they work directly with Miami. They work with New York too. And Marcus keeps it flowing smooth."

I didn't know much about the criminal underworld on the East Coast. The bigger cities were divided up and shared by bosses and families and they controlled the drugs, the prostitution, the gangs, stuff like that. Roanoke, a modest city by comparison, drew an inordinate amount of attention because of its strategic location on the map. Marcus Morgan was the big local player.

"They came here to kill you, honky."

"Who?"

Big Will said, "Them. The Kings weren't so happy about losing the white cop. Sanders. Not so happy about losing Silva either. Not so happy about finding a new transfer station. All your fucking fault, August."

I shrugged, the way Superman does after catching beautiful women falling from burning buildings. "Just so stories about my heroism don't inflate beyond credibility, let's set the record straight. I didn't kill either those two."

"They still blame you. So they sent a couple shooters. I rode along. Professional interest. Nothing personal. Last minute, Marcus talked them out of it."

"Why."

"Marcus say he owed you. Said probably they couldn't kill both you two honkies and the other would come back and bite them in the ass. More fucking trouble than you're worth, two amateurs."

"Sounds like I owe Marcus a cake," I said.

"You're in deep, white man. Deeper than you know. You owe Marcus more than a damn cake."

Manny frowned. "Amateurs? Us?"

ON THE DRIVE HOME, I told Manny, "Second time today I've been told to watch my step."

"Who else?"

"Federal attorney warned me about Calvin Summers. Said Calvin's connected. Not to piss him off."

"You make friends everywhere you go, amigo."

"You cut a deal with Big Will to let his brother go?" I asked.

"Sí."

"That's not how Roanoke marshals usually do things."

"Sí."

"But you're not a typical Roanoke marshal," I said.

"Gonna be here a while. Doing things my way."

"Does Big Will worry you?"

"Big Will, no. Marcus, maybe. The Mafioso, un poco."

"The Mafioso strikes me as overly sensitive," I said. "In reality, we're very likable."

"We? Dios mío. It's you they after, honky."

8

I found Calvin Summer's dairy farm on Google Maps. Just like Philip Marlowe used to do in the fifties. The land was buried in the vast expanse of rolling farm country south and west of Rocky Mount. There were dairy giants nearby but this wasn't one of them. This was a smaller operation.

It struck me as odd. Why would he purchase a dairy farm? It wasn't exactly a classic investment. Staring at the screen, I followed fence lines and small roads which circumnavigated the farm. Memorized the blueprint. Fixed the layout in my mind, especially the partially hidden facility in the back, which caught my eye as being out of place. However, the trip took an hour and as soon as I showed up on site I forgot everything. Google failed to convey the disorienting odor of bovine and I'd misjudged distances. Later on I would circle the lot and probably get lost looking for the odd facility.

The farm's manager, Boyd Hunt, sauntered out to meet me after I'd parked under a maple near the white farmhouse. Probably sixty, wearing overalls, muddy boots, open face, body appeared made from oak.

He shook my hand. "Boyd Hunt."

"Mackenzie," I said. "Nice place."

"Well sir, it's not mine." He chuckled good-naturedly. Aw shucks. "Not any longer. Mr. Summers, as you know, purchased it almost five years ago. But thank you. Take a great deal of pride in it."

The house was surrounded by various sheds and barns, which in turn were surrounded by fenced grassland as far as I could see. Cows dotted all the hills. A collie barked once at me and sat. We walked away from my car and deeper into the complex and into the rich smells of dung.

"Why'd you sell it?" I asked. "Not profitable?"

"Plenty profitable," he said. "But Mr. Summers made me an offer I couldn't refuse, so to speak. Asked the wife and me to stay on as the managers, to live in the same house and keep things running. Paid enough for us to retire but we enjoy the work. The farmhands are like family, you know."

"You didn't want to pass the farm down to family?"

"Was the original plan, yes sir, but we had two daughters. They've both got off to college and moved to cities. Got no interest in taking it over. My grandchildren stare at video game screens all day, no common sense, no work ethic, so...Mr. Summers's offer was a godsend. What's your interest in it?"

"Summers is thinking of expanding," I said. "I'm a consultant."

"Big consultant."

"The boots give me good posture. If I take them off, I'm only five-six."

Boyd Hunt laughed. He probably thought of me as family now too. I couldn't blame him. Everyone wished their son was hilarious.

I said, "Mr. Summers never told me why he bought the farm in the first place. Any idea?"

He paused and took his time answering. "Well, no, not exactly. He grew up around here, so did his daughter, and he said he always wanted a farm. Makes sense but he never comes to visit or work. So who knows."

Boyd showed me the milking barn and briefly expounded on the machinery and threw around some cattle numbers. I studiously wrote everything down. Master of disguise.

"What do you think of his plan to purchase another farm?" I asked.

Another pause. "Got no idea."

"Is it profitable for him, as an investor?"

He rubbed at his weathered forehead with the back of his wrist. "Don't know for sure, but I'd guess...barely. After personnel expenses are paid and after interest and mortgages and insurance, my guess is barely. Farming isn't a lucrative career, much less investing in one. As the owner and operator I did fine, but as a remote investment? Ain't so sure."

"He never comes around?"

"Not for months."

"Do your farmhands even know his name?"

"Oh sure." He sniffed and waved his hand toward the long gravel driveway. "They call him Lexus. When he shows, it's in that silver car. 'Here comes Lexus,' they call."

"Who handles the money?"

"Not me. My wife don't trust me much with numbers. Why we've got a good marriage. She works with his finance guy up Roanoke. Revenue comes in from dairy distributors and she does monthly expenses and I see none of it. Not till it shows in my personal bank account."

We stopped at one of the wide gates. I rested my arms on top and hooked my boot onto the lowest rung. I hoped he noticed how much like John Wayne I looked. "What changes has Mr. Summers made?"

"I don't follow."

"New owners usually tweak their projects. Reduce expenses, that kind of thing."

"Not a one. He asks no questions, makes no demands. Like I said, a godsend."

"Your farmhands feel the same way?" I asked.

"Not initially. They preferred it stay in the family, so to speak."

"Anybody quit?"

"Two boys quit. Been with me fifteen years and they hoped maybe I'd give it to them one day. But a farm is too big a thing to gift away."

I liked Boyd. He didn't have a cell phone that I could see. Easy way of speaking, dirt under his nails, made solid eye contact.

"Mind if I look at your books sometime?" I asked. "I'd like to get a better handle on the numbers before reporting back."

"Have to speak to Mrs. Hunt or his guy up the city. But my wife's visiting grandkids in Raleigh. Back later this week."

We talked a little more and I left. Professional instincts told me that Boyd wouldn't steal to save his life, or rat on his employer to save his wife. But his pauses made me wonder more about the hidden facility I'd seen on Google Earth.

I got back in the Accord and slowly made my way around the entire lot, which was over five hundred acres. Soon the house and sheds were out of sight, lost beyond the hills. An unmarked gravel road separated the Hunt farm from the neighboring lot to the north and I took that road, keeping a close eye on my satellite map.

A quarter mile out, I parked and walked. The air had warmed just enough to encourage the first bees and grasshoppers and I swished against tall grass to keep out of the mud.

It wasn't a facility I'd seen, after all. Or at least it wasn't a network of small buildings. It was a still, built around and amongst the trees. Almost certainly producing moonshine, and lots of it. Enormous steal mash pots, copper distilling heads, multiple hundred-gallon boilers. Only one man was here working but it looked like a big operation. I watched through the cover of trees as he stirred barrels of... probably fruit? I was somewhat less than an expert.

This distillery was illegal. Had to be. Otherwise why hide it? Could Summers have purchased this farm simply to camouflage a moonshine operation? Struck me as a lot of work. But it also seemed like it would produce oceans of shine, a drink in high demand round these parts.

What to do.

What to do.

There was only one guy. He probably couldn't beat me up too bad.

I pushed through the pine and poplar, intentionally causing a ruckus. Stepping on branches. Scuffing the gravel. As I neared, more of the distillery revealed itself. Big damn operation.

The lone worker turned and regarded me, long metal paddle held like a javelin on his shoulder. Tall guy, heavy with muscle. His mouth hung open. He had a thick goatee. Boston Red Sox cap. Beefy forearms.

I took note of his large Chevy truck.

"Could it be," I said, "the notorious Wayne?"

"Who're you," he barked. Had he been a dog, his hackles would be raised.

"Summers didn't tell me you worked at the distillery. Man of many talents."

"You're that fucker's been snooping around."

"Name's Mackenzie. Professional fucker and snooper, hired by Summers to help expand his empire."

"No you ain't."

"I ain't?"

"You're looking for the snitch," Wayne said, throwing his paddle back into the barrel. His boots looked so caked with mud they could hide triceratops fossils. "The hell kinda name is Mackenzie?"

"The elite kind."

"Summers thinks I'm the snitch? Well I ain't."

"I'll tell him so. Surely someone with tires of such impressive height can be trusted."

"You're a got'damn piece of shit, you know that. I ain't ratted out nobody. Neither has my crew."

I briefly debated the merits of explaining double negatives, but Wayne looked bigger and stronger than me (hard to do) and thus I assumed he would not absorb such niceties.

"I'm looking into Summers's affairs, Wayne. Right now I'm learning about the distillery."

"How about you and I cut the shit, Mack. He hired you to find the snitch and waste the bastard. I know better'n most what Summers is into. I know what he's got to hide and I don't cross him."

"What makes you think you know better than most?"

"I'm here, ain't I?" he asked. "Making the shine? He trusts me. And fuck you, that's what."

"Wow. An original and withering invective, Wayne."

"What?"

"Making moonshine isn't impressive, is it? Even Scott at Happy Hills knows about the moonshine."

Wayne scoffed. "Scott don't know shit. We give those dusty corpses the leftovers. They don't get top shelf. Nothing from this place. This here's primo. And I'll tell you one thing. You're lucky I ain't the snitch. 'Cause I had something to hide? And we out here alone? I'd kill you right now."

"Yikes. How on earth would you do such a thing?"

He hit me.

I didn't recognize we'd gotten close enough. I saw the roll of his shoulder at the last instant and pivoted with the punch, but still he rocked me backwards. The lights dimmed and the world had to steady itself.

"How 'bout I just beat you to death, that's how."

"Wayne!" I shouted. "Ouch! This will not look good on my report."

"You can take a punch, I'll give you that. For a narc."

A hot ball of anger was building in my chest. I wanted to knock his teeth out, here and now. Be kinda fun, slugging it out with this heavyweight. I'd pay a thousand dollars for one clean uppercut. But I hadn't been hired to start fights.

Mastering my pride and fury was taking all of me.

I walked a few steps away and ground my teeth.

I hopped a little.

I hadn't been hired to get into fights, I told myself again.

"Jesus," he said. He was staring at the pistol clipped to my belt, small of my back. "You thinking about acing me?"

"Not seriously."

"That a 1911?"

"Yes. Kimber .45."

"Kimber? Never heard of it."

"Used by Los Angeles SWAT," I said.

"Huh."

Wayne had enough intelligence (but only just) to put the pieces together. Realize he hadn't hit a random schmuck. That maybe he'd tried to bully the wrong man, a man who could bully back.

Deep breath.

And another one.

"All right, Mack. Now we understand each other."

"I got a feeling, Wayne, you understand very little. But I'm not so sure my employer would appreciate me pulling your throat out through your nose and driving your truck around town with you strapped to the hood."

"That's how it's gonna be?"

"That's how it's gonna be."

"Summers wasn't messing around, he hired you, boy, but I ain't the snitch. You wanna settle this now?"

"I'm leaving," I said, already on my way out. "I'm trying to turn the other cheek, so to speak, but thinking about shooting you is getting too tempting."

I STARED at the dark television until midnight. An empty beer bottle in my left hand, and an ice pack long since melted in my right. My face throbbed around my left cheekbone and my jaw cracked when I opened it.

Five years ago, I would have killed him.

But I was a new man now.

A man who got decked and did nothing.

That didn't sit well with me. I thought I'd done the right thing; I hadn't retaliated out of emotion or pride. Hadn't killed or maimed him. Hadn't gotten myself hurt further. And yet...

And yet.

I hadn't resolved what to do once I laid bare Calvin's mole. I'd taken the job on impulse, to be near Ronnie, to protect her, to hurt

Calvin's criminal enterprise. Because I didn't like him. But now I liked Wayne less.

My phone buzzed. Another text from Kristin Payne. I should probably reply.

But.

The house's rear staircase creaked. Soft footfalls on the polished hardwood. Someone got a glass of ice water and quietly came into the room with me.

"Hey kiddo," Sheriff Stackhouse said and she ruffled my hair. Like she would do to a six-year-old. Based on periphery clues, I deduced she was wearing her blue nightshirt which hadn't been tailored for modesty. She was as good as fifty got, an inspiring recipe of good breeding and plastic surgery. I kept my eyes straight ahead. Honor thy father and thy father's girlfriend. "How's the face?"

"Chiseled. Handsome. And sore."

"And you didn't hit the guy back," she said.

"I've spent most of the evening wishing I had."

"Why didn't you?"

"Trying to grow up, I suppose. Pretend like I'm more than a Neanderthal," I said. "Take the road less traveled."

"Your father says you're a christian."

"Yeah, some of that too."

"I respect a man who follows through on his convictions. Very strong. Very sexy."

"That's why I let him hit me," I said. "The sex appeal."

She laughed, a husky, throaty sound I worried would wake Kix. "Want me to bring him in for assault?"

I didn't respond.

"Never mind. That was offensive. You can handle yourself, I know."

"Correct," I said.

"What are you going to do about him?"

"I got a feeling he and I will bump heads again. At which point I might take the Neanderthal approach."

"Ooo, may I watch?"

"No. Go back to bed with my father."

"Respect your elders, young man." She gave a clump of my hair a sharp tug and turned to leave. "What do you think? Does your old man have another round in him tonight?"

"Then again, I might let Wayne put me out of my misery."

9

Tom Bradshaw's office was in the Wells Fargo tower downtown. Fourteenth floor with an expansive view of Mill Mountain. His desk was polished and glass trophies proclaiming economic superlatives decorated his shelves. A small television set on a filing cabinet was turned to the golf channel, announcers barely audible.

"Mr. August, come in. He told me you might come by. Please, have a seat. If you can fit, my goodness, that chair's never looked so small," he said, indicating the chair opposite his desk.

"Why are all you finance guys so fit and trim, Mr. Bradshaw?"

"Call me Tom. And weight and calories are numbers, something we monitor closely." He'd gone mostly bald. His shrewd eyes were set narrowly around his nose and he had a way of speaking that hinted at nasal surgery in the past. Argyle sweater vest over a blue button-up.

"Ah," I said.

"And we were too nerdy to make varsity anything, other than cross-country. Also, damn, what happened to your cheek?"

"Walrus."

He laughed. Everyone loves a good walrus joke.

"Did Calvin Summers tell you why he hired me?"

He nodded. "He did. He did. Unfortunate business. How can I help?"

"I'm still getting started. Learning as much as I can. What is your best guess about the nature of the evidence the mysterious informant passed to the federal prosecutor?"

"Can you not ask him that?"

"I can but I'm working this from a different angle."

"If you figure that out, it will narrow down your suspects, right?"

"Bingo." I shot him with my finger.

"I would assume financial information, like receipts or bank statements or figures. Possibly intercepted communication."

"Because Calvin was busted for unclaimed income it's almost certainly something to do with numbers."

"Yes," he said.

"Seems to me, based on that assumption, you ought to be suspect number one."

He smiled and his eye twitched. "I can understand that. But Mr. Summers trusts me. Else I'd no longer have him as a client. And the nature of the, ah, income in question falls outside of my scope of influence."

"Do you know if Ronnie Summers saw the evidence presented against Mr. Summers?"

"I'm sure she did. It is my understanding that she didn't have to see much to realize their best course of action was to accept a plea deal. Again, I assume they presented her with documents detailing illegal finances."

"Finances outside your scope of influence."

"Yes."

"So you were never implicated?" I asked.

"Because I was never complicit."

"But you're the finance guy."

"Not, apparently, for all his endeavors," he said.

"What income had Calvin hidden from the government?"

"I am not privy to that. He's never told me."

"Does he employ a secondary finance guy?"

He shook his head and rearranged the silver pens on his desk. "Not to my knowledge."

"So the hidden income wouldn't be from a legal enterprise. At least not from one of the enterprises you oversee, because you would note the discrepancy."

"Correct. I only deal in, ah, legal commerce."

"So the illegal income in question didn't originate from the rental houses or the trailer parks or the restaurant or the dairy farm?"

"Correct, nor from the convenience stores."

"In other words," I said, wisely, "he generated the money from criminal endeavors."

"Not necessarily. It could be *unclaimed* legal income." He emphasized it heavily because he assumed no one could be as handsome *and* as intelligent as I appeared.

I said, "*Unclaimed* legal income, from something like a banana stand?"

His eyes crinkled with subdued mirth. Very subdued. "Clever. You're funny."

"Correct."

"Here's what I think happened. Again, I wasn't in the room."

"Of course."

He steepled his fingers and spoke over them. "I think the government presented him evidence of significant income which he wasn't claiming, and for the moment let us not concern ourselves with the source. The money was simply there. And the government could prove it. At which point he and his lawyer scrambled for any method to mitigate the legal fallout. They looked for a source which couldn't be traced through paperwork. Often, in cases such as this, the best, ah, solution is to claim it was a gift or even better claim it came from gambling. Neither of which is legal but much better than, say, from human trafficking. Which clearly Mr. Summers does not participate in but I'm using it as an example."

"So they lied about the source of the income."

"Possibly. It happens."

"And the IRS and the federal attorney bought it?" I asked.

"Almost certainly not. But how far down the rabbit hole does the IRS want to go? Or the local federal office? Mr. Summers paid a heavy fine, paid the back taxes, and spent six months in jail. A big win for them. It's the same way the FBI got Al Capone, if I'm not mistaken. They knew he was deep into the underworld but they got him on tax evasion."

"So what else is Mr. Summers into?"

He grinned. "I said we shouldn't concern ourselves with the source of the income."

"I'm super concerned with it."

"I'm afraid I have no idea about the source. Knowing Mr. Summers as I do, I presume it originates from something harmless. Like a gift."

"If I knew, I could catch his informant easier," I said.

"I'm sure you could but you're asking the wrong man."

"Whom should I ask?"

"'Whom'?" His fingers were still steepled.

"I read books sometimes," I said. "And learn stuff. And say fancy things like whom."

"I don't know whom you should ask. Isn't that what you're being paid for?"

"Supposedly. How am I doing so far?"

"At the moment, you're barking up the wrong tree."

"So you don't keep the books on his moonshine business?" I asked.

"Mr. Summers has no moonshine business that I'm aware of." He said it quickly, no hesitation, no surprise.

"Is it lucrative? Selling moonshine?"

A small shrug. "No idea. I've never purchased, sold, or tried it, nor have I worked with anyone in the industry."

"Other than Calvin and many of his employees, you mean."

"Do all private investigators seek to badger and aggravate their sources? Or are you an anomaly?"

"We could call Calvin right now. Get permission for you to talk with me about his moonshine operation?"

"I'm afraid it's a very busy day, Mr. August. And I have other clients coming in. Perhaps we can continue this discussion in the future."

"How large an investment is required for you to take me on as a client?" I asked. "You know, start planning my retirement."

"The minimum I help invest is five hundred thousand dollars."

"I'll come back in seventy-five years."

I KNOCKED on Ronnie's heavy office door and pushed into the receptionist area.

The cute assistant looked up from her enormous desk and said, "It's you."

"It's me. Hello Natasha Gordon."

"I'm afraid Ms. Summers is not here," she said and she managed to look genuinely disappointed.

"Ah. Rotten luck."

"I'll tell her you came by."

"Would you mention that I looked especially dashing and virile today?"

She pretended to write on her notepad. "...especially...dashing. Got it. Is there anything I can help you with in the meantime?"

"Can I borrow four hundred and ninety thousand dollars?"

"Is there anything *else* I can help with?"

"Do you know why Calvin Summers hired me?"

"I do," she said.

"So we can speak candidly."

"I think so."

"What do you think?"

"I think I hope you catch the man who did it. You may sit down, if you want."

I did. The cushions were elite. "Do you work for Mr. Summers?"

"No. I'm an employee of this law firm, not of his investments. However the two businesses are often intertwined."

"How so?"

She bit nervously at her bottom lip. "Am I allowed to talk about this?"

"Sure."

"I'm not sure I believe you. Ms. Summers described you as mischievous."

"She meant inquisitive. Which is my job. Calvin Summers hired me to ask questions. Ergo, I ask. How are the two businesses intertwined?"

"Well, she handles all of Mr. Summers's legal work. Sometimes there is a lot."

"Like what?" I asked.

"Like employment disputes, tax questions, the criminal trial. Plus, Mr. Summers insists she help his friends with their entanglements. Kids caught drunk driving, thinks like that."

"Is Calvin her biggest client?"

"...Yes, I suppose. Technically."

"I detect there's more to your answer."

Unconsciously, her voice dropped to a half whisper. "So Mr. Summers consumes more of her time than any other client. So in that way he is her biggest. But he's not *really* a client. He's family. He doesn't pay her."

"For any of it?"

"None. He forces her to do the work pro bono."

"How does he force her?" I asked.

"Paternal pressure, I suppose."

"Is that fiscally responsible?"

"Ms. Summers isn't poor. But her law firm makes half of what it could," she said.

"Because of him."

"Because of Mr. Summers, yes."

"Are you and Ronnie close?"

Her face brightened. "I hope so, yes. Probably closer than most in our situation. She doesn't have many friends, to be honest."

"Did she talk to you about her father's legal trouble?"

"No."

"She was privy to the evidence presented against her father. Did she mention it?" I asked.

She shook her head, ponytail swaying. "No. I know nothing about it."

"Has Calvin ever been cruel to you?"

"Oh no. He's a perfect gentleman to everyone except his daughter."

"He demands a lot of her."

"Off the record, he's awful to her."

"Families are hard," I said, grinding my teeth, and doing my best to pry my fingers off the armrests. I was about to break them.

"Extremely. Mine too."

"Have you met Wayne?" I asked.

"Wayne?"

"Wayne Cross. Big guy. Works at the trailer parks."

"I know the name. I've never met him. If they don't work with Ms. Summers then I usually don't know much about them. Sorry."

"So you don't know Scott."

"No. Sorry." To her credit, she looked authentically sorry.

"Do you know much about Calvin's rental properties?"

"I don't. Mr. Bradshaw would, though."

"What about the convenience stores?"

"Ask Mr. Bradshaw," she said.

"Does Calvin ever come to this office?"

"Sure, sometimes."

"Does he give out moonshine? Maybe as a Christmas present?"

"Does he give...what? I don't understand. No, he doesn't."

Poor Natasha. She looked as though she was being interviewed by an idiot.

"Have you met Boyd Hunt?" I asked.

"The farmer?"

"Dairy farm operator, yes."

"I knew him when I was a child. I'm still in contact with his wife, who is lovely. Does that help? Very nice woman. She lives in

Franklin County. I used to be friends with her daughter, back in high school."

"Does Mrs. Hunt strike you as a government informant?"

"No. She does not."

"What about Mr. Stokes? Property manager?"

"Yes." A crisp nod, ponytail swaying. "Him I know."

"And?"

"And what?"

"Could he have betrayed Calvin?"

"I don't know. I know he comes in to ogle Ms. Summers as often as he can," she said.

"Ew."

"I think so too."

The door behind me opened. I turned to see a sharply dressed man in a coal black suit. He paused at the doorway. Despite being indoors, he wore black Ray-Bans. His head was shaved and it gleamed and he inclined it curiously toward me and then down to his watch.

Natasha Gordon said, "I'm sorry, Mr. Antoine, but Ms. Summers is out. I'll tell her you came by."

Mr. Antoine didn't speak. I got the impression his eyes were resting on me. I tried to look professionally ferocious.

More silence.

Natasha Gordon fidgeted.

"Am I sitting in your chair?" I asked him.

"This is the second time," Mr. Antoine said. Dark and displeased voice.

"I'm sorry, sir."

"Happens again, I inform Mr. Summers I'm getting a new lawyer. And he don't want to lose my business."

"Yes, I'll let her know. I apologize."

He glared another moment and left. The door clicked softly behind him.

"He's kinda spooky," I said.

Natasha looked as though she was releasing a breath she'd been holding. "Yes."

"One of Calvin Summer's friends whom he foists upon the legal counsel of his daughter?"

"Something like that."

"What's he do?"

"I haven't been told."

"When he's displeased with his attorney he threatens to tattle on her to the father?" I asked.

"It's complicated."

"How soon will Ronnie be back?"

"Not for a few days. She drove to Washington."

Despite my professional ferocity, despite my stalwart spirit and my heart of gold and my strongly controlled emotions, my heart sank. "To visit her fiancé?"

"Yes."

"Have you met him?"

"I have not. I don't believe he's ever been here. He's a federal prosecutor."

"Wow."

"I think so too."

I said, "Thank you for the information."

"Was I much help?"

"Yes. And more pleasant than Wayne."

"Is Wayne what happened to your face?" she asked.

"I plead the Fifth."

"It's okay." She smiled, a warm one. "I'll tell Ms. Summers you looked handsome anyway."

10

My phone buzzed.

>> **hey big guy**

>> **lol**

>> **come over tomorrow 4 lunch?**

>> **meet me at roanoke college?**

The texts were from Kristin Payne, the psychology professor, field hockey coach, and size ten hottie. I hadn't seen her since our date.

Did I want to see her again?

...Mostly.

I possessed enough self-awareness to recognize a kind of raw jealousy lurking in my chest. Ronnie was with her fiancé — perfectly natural. That's where she should be. Except I didn't want her to be there. I wanted her to dump the repugnant asshat.

Was he repugnant? Almost certainly. In comparison to intrepid private cops.

I texted Kristin. Told her I would meet her for lunch, but I didn't mention I'd only be coming to mitigate loneliness caused by another woman.

Careful, Mackenzie. Easy.

You are captain of your ship.

Or something like that.

I slipped the phone back into my pocket and forcefully took my mind off Ronnie.

I was standing on a football field at Patrick Henry High School under a deep blue spring sky. The head coach had contacted me again about being his defensive coordinator but this time he suggested I come watch a practice. It was a dirty tactic; the pads and the grass and the whistles hit me like a shot of adrenaline. He'd essentially opened the door to a time machine, whisking me back to halcyon days.

I thought about suiting up and tackling these mere mortals.

This wasn't a real practice though. Those wouldn't start till summer. More or less, the players were running through orchestrated conditioning drills in pads during their off-season. Still. I loved it.

Jeriah Morgan burst through his offensive line, put a fancy move on the nearest linebacker, and sprinted up the field. Jeriah was a former student of mine, a sophomore starting on varsity, a running back with college potential. He caught sight of me and jogged close.

"August! What up, Teach! Haven't seen you."

"Jeriah." I nodded. "Still got the quick feet?"

"You know it."

"You're wasting too much time going east to west."

That stopped him. "Do what?"

"Just now. To elude that linebacker, you went lateral. Can't do that in a game. You'll get caught from behind."

"Yeah, well. What do you know? Can't run over the dude. He's got fifty pounds on me."

"You only need inches in the open field. Change direction, blow by him, not around him. Force him into an arm tackle. You'll get through, most times," I said.

"What, you the coach now?"

"Maybe."

"Yo, August, that'd be lit. You *gotta* be a coach for us."

"We'll see."

He jogged back to the heaving mass of helmets and coaches.

Though madness, there be method in it. They regrouped and ran more plays, keeping lungs and legs hot.

A tall man came onto the field and stopped beside me. Bald, strong, imposing, like black Jason Statham in a suit. He smelled good.

"I been telling the boy, eliminate the fancy maneuvers," Marcus Morgan grumbled. "He don't listen to me. Not anymore. Perhaps he'll attend you."

"Possibly you've reached the stage of fatherhood where you're more obstacle than mentor," I said.

"Lately it's like a competition." He sighed, a deep rush of wind. "Father and son. Trying to prove he's better than me."

"Good to see you, Marcus."

"Been hoping you'd show. This team needs something. Needs you."

We silently watched the practice. When I realized we both had our hands clasped behind our backs I crossed my arms instead. How embarrassing.

"Haven't seen you at church," he said.

"What's a gangster like you go to church for?"

"Not a fucking gangster. I'm a business man. You know this. And what does that have to do with church?"

"I apologize," I said. "You're right. But as soon as I'm without sin, I'm going to throw stones at you."

His stoicism cracked. A pleased smile. "Moving cocaine is no worse than moving sugar. It's illegal but it's a product. Someone will move it, might as well be me. I'm merely the most humane cog in the machine."

"An episcopal cog."

"Episcopal." He sniffed with displeasure. "Denominations are a formality. Hate them. See, I recognize there's more to life than this. Than what we observe. And so I chase it. As best I can any given moment. I'm not episcopal. I am spiritual."

"A spiritual cocaine mover."

"Thankfully you and I, Mr. August, happen to serve a merciful God."

"Amen."

"Amen." He nodded.

I glanced behind him. Sitting on the bleachers was a fat man in jeans. He wore a shirt far too big, probably to hide a gun.

"You got a walk-around guy, now?" I asked.

"A precaution. Became necessary."

"Uh-oh. You angered someone, Marcus. Hard to imagine."

"Apparently I reached a certain rank in the hierarchy of success. Made me a target," he said. "Bodyguard is worth the expense."

"Big Will told me I owe you one."

"Do indeed. Though it was partially self-preservation. They murder you and missed your Mexican friend, he'd come after me."

"You're talking about Manny," I said.

"Yes, Manny."

"Yeah, he'd kill you. And your cute bodyguard."

"I tried to purchase Manny. Seems uninterested in money."

"He didn't tell me that," I said.

"My impression, he marches to the beat of his own drum. And though he's got great affection for you, he is not, ah, beholden to you."

"Yes."

"He strikes me as…incorruptible isn't the right word. Perhaps unmanageable is better. By me or by his superiors."

"Manny does what he wants and he does it well," I said.

"You two make quite the duo. Large personalities in our city."

"So now Sergeant Sanders is gone, you're looking for other cops to put on the payroll," I said.

"Essentially. Cop or marshal, whatever. But he is too principled."

"Not principled. It's survival instincts. A loathing of attachments. He can't let himself be in your debt."

Jeriah jogged past, back to the scrum, giving his father and me an extra long inspection.

"Boy's good," I said.

"Yes. Could be great, but he's got no fight. Just arrogance. What do I do, Mr. August? It's our wealth makes him lazy. I need to live in poverty so he gets a work ethic? The conditions I grew up in made me strong. Made me a man. So I could provide a better life for my wife and my son. But now those conditions make them soft. It kills me. You understand."

"Somewhat. My kid still wears diapers. Men like you and I, we emerged into this world potty trained."

"I was Jeriah's age, I had two jobs. I provided for myself and others," he said, ignoring how funny I was. "Didn't stare at fucking screens all day."

"You want him to take over the family business?"

"Hell no. Shit no. I want him to be a teacher. A surgeon. A defense lawyer. A grocery manager. Something to be proud of. Not like me."

"Not like you."

"You want your boy to grow up and be a detective? Private or otherwise?"

"I do not."

He nodded. "You see."

"That's just the way of things. We hope our children experience no conflict. But that's impossible. It's the conflict which matures us. Can't be a good football players without years of bruising."

He grunted.

I continued, "But I agree — Jeriah should become something other than a gangster."

He sniffed. "Told you. I'm a businessman."

"A businessman working with the District Kings."

"You know about the Kings," he said.

"I know enough."

"I went to a high council meeting, to explain your mess couple months ago," he said.

"They actually call them high council meetings?"

"District Kings aren't thugs. They are educated men."

"And a bit theatrical, I note."

"Damn right," he said. "Men from Latin America. Men from Russia. Europe. America's cities. Dangerous men. Fucking angry men who don't agree on much. But one thing they got in common? They hate you."

"I'm flattered."

"Met in Philadelphia. They sent a squad down immediately. For you," he said.

"Big Will wanted to ride along. To watch the shootout."

"Big Will...he's unique."

"Thanks for convincing the squad otherwise."

"Pay me back. Be in my son's life. Coach this team," he said.

"All right."

"All right?" he said.

"Sure. Be fun."

"Good," he said. "And come to a poker game tonight."

"A poker game."

"Mm-hmm."

"You and I, Marcus, we have a weird co-existence. Call it a friendly truce. But I don't know that means we play cards together. I'm not your ally."

"I know this. Not trying to recruit you into the underworld."

"Mafioso at this game?"

"Maybe. Mostly local guys. Most in Roanoke would kill to get invited," he said.

"Who plays?"

"Calvin Summers."

"You jest."

"Shit you not, August."

"He hired me," I said.

"I know."

"You and he work together?"

"Calvin is a...competitor. To be polite."

"You went to Princeton," I said.

"I did."

"Where'd he go?"

"White-guy dumbass school, my guess," he said.

"Okay. I'll play pinochle with you."

"Poker. I'll text you the address."

"You still got my number?"

"Keeping a close eye on you, August. Closer than you think. Course I got your number."

"I pay my taxes. Obey the speed limit. Always use fertilizer. What are you worried about?" I said. "Why do I need supervision?"

"I talked the Kings outta acing you."

"So?"

"Deal was, you get outta line, I do it myself."

"Ah," I said. "What a dreadful episcopal you are."

I PUT Kix to bed and left for the sinister card game. The address led to the fifth floor of one those downtown buildings without an obvious entrance, just a door in a wall, no markings, the kind of building you only notice at a distance but never up close. I followed the noise upstairs and on the fifth floor I met the corpulent guy I'd seen earlier with Marcus. He still wore the voluminous shirt, hung almost to his knees. His feet were planted, blocking my path, and he regarded me coolly.

"Would you like to buy Girl Scout cookies?" I asked. "I sell enough, my troop wins the vacation."

"The hell is wrong with you."

"Can't you recognize a card sharp when you see one?"

"Sharp?" He frowned, which pressed a lot of flesh together at his eyes. "Thought it was shark."

"Either way. Go ask Marcus if I'm allowed in."

"No need," said Marcus Morgan, appearing at the big guy's elbow. "He with me, Fat Susie."

"Fat Susie," I repeated.

"Got a problem?" asked Fat Susie, in a voice pitched higher than Marcus's.

"Yeah. Your name. You're not that fat."

He tried not to smile, but failed.

Mackenzie August, professional comedian.

Marcus led me down the hall. This floor was vacant and most doors were covered with heavy plastic tarps. The overhead lights were exposed fluorescent bulbs and our voices caromed. "Two games tonight. One down the end a bunch of white guys talking stocks and mutual funds. Boring as hell. We play in here."

He led me into an unfinished room framed with drywall and subfloor. Like the construction budget ran out halfway through. To compensate, it'd been furnished with a rug, a felt poker table, and leather chairs. Drinks in the corner — glasses and scotch. A blue-tooth speaker played Sinatra. Men of gravity and money had already arrived.

"Look at this guy. The gumshoe hero." Calvin Summers stood from his place at the table, his drink in his left hand. He wore a white sports jacket, salmon shirt beneath with a popped collar. Perfect hair perfectly parted. We shook hands. "Good to see you, August. You've found my rat, I hope?"

"In fieri. Soon."

"In fieri?"

Marcus Morgan said, "Means 'In progress,' Summers. Learn your Latin." Morgan pointed at the hirsute lout next to Summers and said, "You met Wayne?"

I said, "I've met Wayne Cross. And his truck. Huge fan of both."

Wayne had dead eyes. He wore a red-checkered flannel shirt. I debated punching him.

Marcus kept going. "You know Big Will." He indicated the bald and bearded man who would sit next to him.

I nodded. "I follow Big Will on Instagram. Love what he does with his corpses."

Big Will, ever my fan, rolled his eyes and continued to shuffle a deck of cards. He did not stand.

The man at the end, the one with a big red face and blue jean jacket, stuck out his hand. "I'm the redneck," he said. "Name's Clay Fleming. From Floyd County."

"Good to meet you, Clay."

Marcus pointed to the man between Wayne and Clay. "This is Edgar Knight. It's his building. Local gun store proprietor, too."

Edgar looked like a land shark. His goatee was well trimmed and pointy. So was his hair, which had lines cut into the sides. Despite being indoors, he wore dark glasses. Dark skin and a dark black suit, and he reminded me a little of Antoine from Ronnie's office but this was a different dude. He nodded at me, didn't offer his hand. "You play cards?"

"I dabble."

"Last player," Marcus said, pointing at the man sitting across from me, next to Calvin Summers. "This is Duane. Colleague down from Washington."

Duane looked like Euro muscle. Strong neck. Muscles bulging at his suit as though it'd been tailored that way. "How you doing," he said. He looked European but he sounded like Jersey, a soft voice. He watched me and his eyebrow arched without amusement. Duane had brought a guy with him, a white guy in a navy suit, tattoos on his neck. Tattoo Guy stood behind Duane's chair.

What a strange crew. Going around the table...

Me — fearless detective

Marcus — cocaine mover

Big Will — streetwise thug

Duane — from Washington, colleague with Marcus

Calvin Summers — rich white guy, ex-con

Wayne — big guy, not as rich, hit me once

Edgar Knight — gun store owner

Clay Fleming — redneck from Floyd County

Why had I been invited?

"Fat Susie, this room is full," Marcus told the big man at the door. "No one else."

Fat Susie nodded.

Each player bought in for five hundred. We handed our money to Edgar, who made neat notes on a ledger. We selected colorful chip denominations from a rich mahogany box under the watchful eye of Edgar and everyone else, denominations totaling five hundred. The game began in silence, nothing but the clacking of chips and the snap hiss of shuffling cards.

Duane won the first two hands with strong bets. He didn't announce the bets; he quietly slid in a stack of chips totaling ninety both times. Aggressive. Rich men folded like he was betting a million. It wasn't about the amount. Ninety dollars was nothing to them. It was about the pride. The shame of starting on even footing and playing bad, losing ground because of poor decisions. This was mere change to them. But having your chips taken away because you were an idiot? That was everything.

Calvin Summers broke the silence. "August. Got any leads?"

He sat across from me. I glanced from him to Wayne and back. "Talk about this here?"

"Wayne knows. I informed him. If you need assistance, you can ask Wayne."

"In that case," I said. "Wayne. I need a drink. Fetch."

The table enjoyed this. Especially Big Will. He wheezed with laughter.

Wayne did not. He tried to hammer my soul with the impact of his dead stare. I remained undaunted.

"Hey," Calvin Summers said. "We have a guest. Get the man a drink. Let's show some hospitality."

With infinite reluctance and silent protest, Wayne acquiesced. He went to the drink station.

"What's August doing for you, Summers?" Clay asked and he began dealing the next set of cards. Quiet flips, corners skimming the felt.

Calvin Summers said, "You already know. Someone in my organization passed incriminating evidence to the government. August is finding the guy."

Wayne returned and set a glass on the table. Far out of my reach. I let it sit.

"Hey. Paul Bunyan," Edgar barked. "Get your fucking drink off my felt."

"It's his drink."

"Move it. Now. You leave a ring, Imma bust you in your nose."

With even greater reluctance, Wayne slid the drink closer to me.

"Thanks Wayne," I said. "Next time just one cube."

Clay Fleming the redneck pointed at me and then at Summers. Back and forth with his finger. "We can talk business? While August's here?"

"You can," Marcus Morgan said. He owned the deepest voice at the table and he remained static and constant in his chair.

"You sure about the dick?" Wayne said. "Fucker's a former LA SWAT guy. A cop."

"Dick is slang for private investigator," I said. "Wayne is merely being collegial."

"That true?" said Duane, the colleague from Washington. His voice was soft like a rasp. Only he and I were in the hand. He bet, I folded. "You former SWAT?"

"More or less."

"More or less," Duane repeated. Gently, like someone who doesn't have to yell.

"I was LAPD. Trained with the SWAT guys. Preferred detective work."

Clay Fleming the redneck looked at Summers, at me, at Duane, then back to Marcus. Looking for help. "So...?"

Marcus said, "August's good. I say he's good, he's good."

"We can talk?"

"We can talk."

"This the white guy aced Sanders?" Edgar said.

Morgan replied, "Technically *I* aced Sanders. But yeah."

"Sanders used to sit that seat, August."

"Lucky me," I said.

"This the white guy working with Sheriff Tits," Edgar said. He indicated me with his chin.

Clay Flemings from Floyd thought this was funny.

So did Big Will. Another wheeze.

"Working with the sheriff," Duane repeated, as he seemed prone to do.

"I said he's good," Marcus Morgan rumbled.

"You say he's good." Edgar shrugged, nonplussed. He had the air of a man requiring greater assurances.

"It's like they don't trust me," I noted.

"August," Marcus sighed. "How do I make my money?"

"Nude modeling, I assume. And moving cocaine."

Laughter. Infinite mirth. I am the best.

"You see. I trust him. August owes me," Marcus said. "He's good for it. A better man than all you. You can talk."

"Yeah. Well," Calvin Summers said. "Just find the guy, August."

Cards were flying. I still hadn't won anything.

I asked, "How do you know the informant's not Wayne?"

"Because it ain't me, motherfucker," Wayne said.

"Elite badinage, Wayne. I meant, other than that."

"It could be Wayne," Summers said. "You got proof?"

Beside me, Marcus was chuckling about badinage.

I said, "Neither proof nor accusation. Inquiring after your certitude, only."

"I doubt it's Wayne. But you should verify," Summers said.

"Ain't me," Wayne grumbled. "I'm loyal."

"Yes you are, Wayne. But, trust and verify."

I asked, "Could it be a family member?"

"Like my fucking attorney?"

"I doubt it's Ronnie. Some other family?"

"No. No other close family," Calvin said.

"One of the guys in this room?" I asked.

Collectively, the room smiled. Like a lion pride smiles.

Calvin shrugged. "Maybe. First though you should eliminate suspicion from my employees."

Duane the colleague from Washington spoke, the soft rasp. Not like the Godfather. Like strength in abeyance. "I doubt it's someone in this room."

"Why's that?" Calvin asked.

"We do not enjoy working with police."

"That's the damn truth."

"Although," Duane said. "I must admit. This Sheriff Tits sounds intriguing."

Clay Fleming let fly. "God almighty, you should see this woman. Like she's elected by Hugh Hefner. Has to be the best-looking sheriff in A-merica. Has to be. Ain't no doubt."

"Might need to meet this sheriff."

"Careful, gentlemen," said Marcus in his deep rumble. "The sheriff in question is dating August's old man."

Marcus, with no germane words spoken between them, took a large pot of chips off Calvin Summers. Summers liked to call and lose, a feckless player.

Duane said, "Dating the sheriff. More I learn about you, the more interesting you become."

"I'm also a ten handicap," I said. "And show no signs of male pattern baldness."

"You do this thing for Summers maybe I got some work for you."

"If it's within the scope of private investigation, I'm your man."

"You do a little violence?"

"I do not. I'm not a thug for hire."

"Not a thug for hire." Duane repeated the words much slower than I'd said them. "What do you do?"

"The stuff cops can't or won't. On the side of decency."

Big Will, without looking up, said, "He works with the spic. Manny the marshal. Couple'a Robin Hoods."

"Manny is from Puerto Rico and we're more like Wyatt Earp and Doc Holiday. Though there's some discussion on who gets to be Wyatt."

"Gets to be Wyatt," Duane said. "Law keepers."

I shrugged. "Friend to the friendless. Hope for the hopeless. Noble hearted. Compared to you guys, I'm Abraham Lincoln."

"Do-Gooders. Marcus, you brought Do-Gooders to this game."

"This game fills up with nothing but drug runners be a boring game," Marcus said. "Variety. Spice of life. Shit like that."

Edgar the gun store owner spoke. "I hear the new marshal's unhinged. A lunatic. You trust him?"

"With my life," I said. "But I'm on his side."

"What side's that."

"The side of decorum. Harmony. Peace and love and Jesus, stuff like that."

"Christ," said Duane. "Couple of fairy princesses."

Big Will scoffed, "Los Angeles made him gay, maybe."

"Los Angeles was an education," I said. "Now I know."

"Now you know. Now you know what?"

"Now I know I'm good at violence but don't enjoy it. That I'd rather be a decent human. And I also know your boys aren't good enough."

Marcus sniffed a quiet laugh. "Avoid violence. Last fall you knocked Nate Silva senseless and shot two his guys."

"Yes. But. I only half-enjoyed it."

"Wait." Duane held up his hand. "Your boys aren't good enough. The fuck's that mean?"

"Fat Susie. Tattoo Neck, the guy behind you. They aren't good enough," I said.

The cards were momentarily forgotten. The awkward silence lasted three heartbeats longer than it should.

"Not good enough. Elaborate. Educate us," said Duane.

"Tattoo Neck is scary looking. Fat Susie is big. But so what?" I said. "Tattoo's got his hands in his pockets. Fat Susie's gun is buried under an entire department store of shirt. If there was trouble, how would I pass the time waiting for them to get their guns?"

More silence. I leaned back in my chair.

"I'm going to pull my gun," I said. "And even with advanced warning your boys will be too slow."

Big Will tensed. Clay squirmed.

Duane arched the eyebrow.

My gun came out. Easy practiced movement. Aimed at Tattoo Neck. Fat Susie didn't move but Tattoo jumped and fished for his pistol within the depths of his jacket.

"Bang," I said.

When he finally got his gun out mine was put away and I was shuffling cards.

"You guys aren't small time," I said. "I know you're not. But guys who like violence? They aren't always the baddest men in the room. I've been doing this a while. Was trained for years. The only person in here ready for me was Big Will. He pulled his gun and no one saw. Anyway. Like I said. Your boys aren't good enough."

Duane the powerful colleague from Washington shot Tattoo Neck an accusing stare and Tattoo put his piece back into his jacket. Then he thought again, decided maybe it should be out. So he put his hand in his jacket. And stood uncomfortably. Poor Tattoo.

Big Will's gun rested on the table, inches from his hand. He watched me with a bored expression but he wasn't bored.

"See," said Marcus Morgan. "Spice of life. Game's livened up already."

"Big Will. My man," Edgar the gun store owner said. "No guns on the table."

Big Will put it away.

Duane took a breath, held it, and said, "Marcus, you told me he was a pain in the ass."

"Wasn't wrong, was I."

"So. Pain in the ass from California. You want to work with me or not?" Duane said.

"Depends on the work."

He and I were in a hand together. I had two sevens in my hand and another seven landed on the board, giving me a set. Very hard to beat. He bet big.

I did nothing. Thought it over. Or pretended to.

"I'll put you on retainer," Duane said. "You do the work I send down."

"I'll pass."

"You'll pass," he said.

I raised him for all my chips.

He watched me.

I remained impassive.

He glanced at the pile of chips, which represented about six fifty. Glanced to Marcus and back to me.

"You'll pass," he said again.

Wayne chuckled. Under his breath he called me a fucking idiot.

Wayne might be right. That was my grocery money on the table.

Duane counted chips and slid them into the middle. He called me. Now the pot was over a thousand.

I turned over three 7s.

Wordlessly he tossed his cards away.

I won. He was down to a hundred.

Clay Fleming the redneck whistled. "Christ almighty."

"You'll pass," Duane said again.

"You and I. We're in different lines of work," I said, stacking the chips in front of me.

We played another hand. In silence.

Duane was the big shot at the table. Almost certainly he sat at high councils with the District Kings. His dominance was assumed by everyone there, including by himself. So the table waited, wondering how he'd react to my rebuff. To losing to me.

Even Fat Susie looked concerned.

"And my boys aren't good enough," Duane said softly.

"Tattoo isn't. Maybe you got him on special?"

"Damn, August." Edgar, guy who looked like a shark in a suit, shook his head. "Most new guys keep their fucking mouth shut first few games."

"No," said Duane. "No. I like August. I like this Do-Gooder. This fairy princess Robin Hood got a big swinging dick."

"Well." I shrugged modestly. "Bigger than Wayne's, anyway."

Again, Clay and Big Will thought this was a riot. Fat Susie chuckled in the corner.

Duane adjusted in his seat and crossed his legs. "Stay alive, August. Don't stick your fucking head into Marcus's business, like with Silva and Sanders."

"Ah, there's the rub," I said. "We're on opposite sides of this thing. I'm a Do-Gooder. You guys are...Do-No-Gooders."

"You don't want to get on the wrong side of me, August," Duane said.

"I am full of fright and dismay."

He clucked his tongue a few times, softly of course, and shook his head. "And I got a feeling most guys don't want to get the wrong side of you."

Big Will said, "Worse than that. Sheriff Tits got the hots for him." He was staring at his chips with disinterest, his cheek resting on his hand, elbow on the table. "And Manny the spic Robin Hood be a pain in the ass, too. Be better we all make nice. Else be a big damn mess."

"Jesus, August." Calvin Summers chuckled and he finished his drink. "I hired you to find my informant. Didn't know I was stepping into a hornet's nest."

"Hornet's nest comes free of charge," I said.

But he was right. This had turned into a mess.

Ronnie was worth it.

11

Against my better judgement I thought about Ronnie and her repugnant fiancé for an hour before falling asleep. The next morning I went jogging with Kix in his stroller and listened to loud music and afterwards I took a cold shower and got ready for my date.

At noon, I followed Kristin Payne's texted directions to her classroom on Roanoke College's campus. One of those small instructional auditoriums with stacked seating to the back. She was chatting with two underclassmen, boys clearly enamored with her tight button-up shirt and the black skirt which didn't reach her knees. She stood barefoot, high heels tossed in the corner. On the professor scale of attraction, starting at Madeline Albright and going up to ten, she was probably an eleven. Which I would only notice if I objectified women, which I didn't. I sat in her swivel chair near the board and spun in a circle.

As promised, she'd brought hamburgers and fries, still steaming in the bag. More likely she'd sent an undergrad to fetch them.

She ushered the two amorous boys out. Closed the door. Locked it.

"Is there a website or app to rate your professor?" I asked. "Like a hot-or-not for teachers?"

"Kinda," she said. She closed the blinds on the door's window, sealing us in. "I do very well on those sites."

"I imagine. I looked in all the doors down the hall. You're lapping the field. Want to eat?"

"Yes," she said. "But first."

It happened quickly. She tugged at my belt. I summoned willpower, any reason to resist, and came up empty. Never let yourself get too lonely, but I had. She had my pants down. Her skirt bunched up around her waist. She wore nothing underneath.

She faced me, straddled me, lowered onto my lap, and the swivel chair rocked backwards ten degrees. Her breath quickened.

"Sorry for sexually assaulting you," she said, a deep husky sigh. "But I've been thinking about this for days."

She unbuttoned her white shirt all the way down. Raised and crossed her wrists over her head. Closed her eyes.

I knew that later I would have mixed emotions.

At the moment, however, higher thought didn't feel possible. Base reptilian instincts had taken over.

HALF AN HOUR later I ate lunch in a different chair, feeling a little off-kilter as though recovering from an out-of-body experience.

She sat next to me, her feet crossed and resting on my thigh. Her white shirt was held in place, only just, by a single button.

"Sex and burgers," she said. "Like we're prehistoric cave dwellers."

"I'm going to put that in your reviews on the professor rating website," I said.

"Going to mention my other skills?"

"I'll include that you're thoroughly groomed. And that your dead lift is impressive."

"Damn right it is." She grinned. "Haven't you always wanted to bang a professor?"

"We went to college together. Do you not remember them? I am aghast at the thought."

"None of them had my quads, though."

"Dr. Williams might have. But he was irritable."

She laughed.

I tried to shake off the drunken feeling.

"How's your burger?" she asked.

"You're right. Sex and burgers go hand in hand somehow."

"You can grill for me next time, afterwards. I like bacon mixed in with my beef," she said. She had a habit of talking around bites of food, as though her aggression spilled into her dining.

"All our sexual encounters seem to happen inside college facilities. No grills here."

"Shame. Are you working on anything interesting now?"

"Yeah. A big family mess which gets messier the further I go," I said.

"Tell me about it. I have a degree in psychology, you know."

"The girl hired me, she's verbally abused by her father. Maybe in other ways too. She's an adult. Smart. Strong. But allows herself to be bullied by her old man. I'm caught in the middle."

"Oof. That's tough. You should probably keep your yap shut about it while you're in her employ. The last thing she needs is a doofus like you judging her."

"Doing my best. And you need your tuition back, if years of clinical training taught you I'm a doofus."

"Your client probably feels as though she has no right to resist. Kids bestow upon parents the essence of 'rightness.' Parents are right and good, and so what they do therefore is right and good. It carries over into adulthood. Plus, how many grown-ups do you know who have completely cast aside their parents? It's hard. The guilt would be brutal."

"But possibly worth it."

"That's easy for us to say, as outside observers. Girls are weird, Mack. I had functional and affectionate parents and I still have issues.

Keep your professional and personal life separate, my advice," she said.

"Speaking of professional life, I need to go spy on people."

"I'll give you a tour of the campus before you go. We can hold hands and listen to the birds, like a real couple."

"Sounds great."

She stood and smoothed her skirt and buttoned the rest of her shirt.

"No," she said. "No. That's not fair. I molested you, not the other way round, and I was feeling sentimental about it. But I can separate the physical from the emotional. I shouldn't have asked for more. You don't need to walk with me."

"Not like it'd be a chore, walking with a pretty girl."

"No. Just go. But make sure you ask me out again."

"For dinner. I'll cook for you."

"Bingo, buster. And make it snappy."

12

I was in luck. Wayne was still at home at one in the afternoon. Lazy bastard.

He lived in a one-story brick ranch set awkwardly on the side of a hill and overhung with towering trees and dangling dormant kudzu. His personal bend in the road afforded no view of neighbors, limiting my stakeout location potential, so I parked a quarter mile down the road. If he went to the dairy farm or into town, I'd see it.

I'd recently run into Adam Moseley, a local attorney and guardian ad litem and Navy JAG, and he'd recommended a book called *Hillbilly Elegy* for understanding the parts of Franklin County which baffled me — the parts which were poor and proud of it. A significant chunk of the population defiantly refused progress and spat in the face of success. Poverty was the family tradition. To paraphrase the author, they encouraged social decay instead of fighting against it.

And I didn't get it.

So I read. And read.

And grew despondent, thinking about the kids growing up in houses with decomposed floors and the parents who were pleased with the rot. Generational brokenness. Most of Franklin County wasn't this way; most folk were hard-working and prosperous and a credit to the county. But "Redneck Appalachia" had a strong presence here, a stone around society's neck, and it wasn't getting better.

As was usually the way, the problems went deeper than sheer stupidity and had a lot to do with the decline of working-class jobs. Being an outsider, the book informed me, meant that my pious and self-righteous opinions would fall on deaf ears was I stupid enough to express my "enlightened" point of view.

After two hours of reading I decided I should keep my mouth shut about their backwards ways.

And also about Ronnie's familial trauma. I couldn't stop thinking about her and Calvin's verbal abuse. But. I was an outsider, not family, and it wasn't my place to intervene. That was Kristin's counsel and it was solid advice.

Maybe.

Or maybe not. Kristin struck me as the kind of girl who was more contrived than levelheaded. She ran on instinct and impulse and aggression.

I'd already forgotten about our pre-lunch tryst — my first such encounter in over two years. It'd been hot. It made for a titillating memory. Yet, I felt no grand satisfaction, no slaking of corporeal desire. I was unassuaged.

Shouldn't I be more...something? Content? Gratified? But I wasn't. Which meant what?

That the encounter didn't mean anything.

That it was misguided.

That it was with the wrong girl.

And, per usual, that it was going to end badly.

Or maybe, August, maybe you should just enjoy having sex with the hot girl. What kinda lousy private detective are you? Marlowe would be ashamed.

No. It was going to end badly. Professional hunch.

Also, what kind of ostentatious prick thinks in terms like "ersatz succor"? I needed to read less and watch Netflix more, lest I grow sick of my own pretentiousness.

Wayne drove past at three. Had I not seen his truck I'd have detected him via his ludicrous muffler. Clearly overcompensating for a slight by mother nature and father Cross. I gave him a lead and pursued. He drove deep into Callaway, where my shiny Honda Accord looked as natural and as native as a purple unicorn. Ridden by Katy Perry. I hung back but if he was looking for a tail then he'd spot me easily. Nothing to be done.

He pulled onto an unmarked dirt road off Route 752. Again I parked at a distance and lay in wait. I located the plot of land on my phone's map and with my considerable skills of detection I was able to discern exactly nothing. Whatever it was back there, it'd been hidden effectively within a canopy of foliage.

Thirty minutes later he emerged. His truck bed brimmed with haystacks tied down.

Haystacks?

I was perplexed.

But I gave chase, following the devious farmer on his clandestine mission to feed wicked cows. Good thing I was wasting my afternoon, following him instead of playing with my son.

Our path ran north and east toward Rocky Mount and he pulled into Happy Hills, the trailer park from hell. I parked on the highway half a mile past and jogged back in time to witness Wayne and Scott unloading supplies (they'd been hidden in the haystacks, obviously) and carrying them into a trailer, which was most likely used for storage.

"Ah hah," I said. I was concealed in the tree line and didn't have binoculars so I couldn't be sure but I assumed the supplies hidden in the hay were jugs of moonshine. I'd already known Wayne was providing Happy Hills with "shine," which meant I'd learnt nothing of note, but saying "Ah hah" made me feel better.

However! I'd located another of Calvin Summer's moonshine stills. Ah hah.

I returned to my Accord and waited. Soon Wayne howled past and we motored out of Rocky Mount.

I turned on the radio to drown out his muffler. Didn't work.

He pulled into another trailer park. This was Calvin Summer's third, the one I hadn't visited yet, called Glade Hill Acres. A grassy plot dotted with pine trees and single-wides. The intersecting roads were broken pavement. No dogs. No rusted-out cars. Glade Hill Acres fell somewhere between the upper-middle class Ferrum's Fields and the decrepit Happy Hills. Wayne parked at a unit near the back and began to unload. He was joined by a man who half-jogged and half-limped from a nearby unit. They finished and Wayne left, roaring away in his Tonka. He never glanced my way, the adenoidal chunk of flannel.

I eased my Accord into Glade Hill Acres and parked at the storage trailer. A handful of tenants stood at their screen doors and watched. I consulted the list of names Ronnie had provided and I got out.

The storage trailer was accessed by a wooden ramp instead of stairs. The windows were shut and boarded. The door had two locks and an alarm system. Wayne wasn't taking chances.

I walked around the unit and saw no simple way in.

"'Scuse me!"

The man was returning, limping and wincing. Upon a closer inspection he looked sixty, mostly bald. He wore a bathing suit and flip-flops and his left foot was purple. His face was plain and not un-friendly.

"'Scuse me," he called again. "This's private property. Help you?"

"Yeah, I'm supposed to meet Wayne." I walked to him, fists on my hips. "But I'm running a little late. My fault, not his. I got lost."

"Wayne? Wayne just left."

"How long ago?"

"Five minutes, maybe."

"Damn. I'll give him a call. Maybe he'll come back," I said.

"Are you police?"

I grinned.

"No. I'm a consultant working with Calvin Summers. You know him?"

"Sure." He nodded and scratched his scalp. "Sure, yeah, sure. He's the owner. Who're you?"

"Mackenzie. Mr. Summers hired me to upgrade Glade Hill Acres and a few of his other properties. I was supposed to help Wayne unload. You know, learn how the distribution works."

"Oh, okay," he said. His mouth naturally hung open and his expression bordered on bewilderment. "Okay, yeah. What distribution?"

"Wayne said he was bringing supplies. Moonshine, things like that. Told me to meet him at the unit in the back so I could see for myself. He already unloaded?"

"Yes sir. Yes sir he did and I helped him."

"You helped? You're not Keith Bradley, are you?"

The man's face changed from confusion to pleasure. "Sure am. I'm Keith."

"Then you're the superintendent." I stuck out my hand and he shook it.

"Yep, that's me, I'm the super."

"He told me you were a handy guy."

"He did? Wayne said that?"

"You're the expert, maybe you can help me," I said. Keith enjoyed being referred to as an expert. "I'll be making recommendations to Mr. Summers soon about the nature of Glade Hill Acres. What improvements should we focus on first?"

"Huh. Not sure I follow."

"What needs fixing? Based on first inspection, I'd guess the roads."

"Oh okay, sure, I see. Naw, roads are fine. It's the tree roots, what digs them up."

"Water is good? Sewers work?"

"Sure, yeah, sure. Everything works. This place is nicer than any of us is used to," Keith said.

"What do you mean?"

"Well, you know, hard for us to find nice places to live. Everyone gets so antsy."

"When you say 'us,' who are you referring to?"

"Huh?" he said.

"Who lives here? Who has a hard time finding a nice place to stay?"

"The sex offenders. Wayne ain't tell you?"

"No he didn't," I said. "Neither did Mr. Summers."

"Everyone lives here, we're sex offenders. I'm not ashamed. Leastways I married her, soon as I could. People here are good folks."

"Why...how...I guess I'm confused. Every resident of Glade Hill Acres is a registered sex offender?"

He nodded and eased the weight off his purple foot. "Yes sir, pretty sure."

"What's the purpose of catering solely to sex offenders?"

"We make great tenants. You know? Already got a strike against us so we play it safe. Gotta live somewhere. Besides, who else would live here? People believe us monsters. So we stick together."

"How many of the residents here sign government checks over to Wayne?"

"'Bout half."

"And that's the half who get the moonshine," I said. "The moonshine he keeps stored in the supply unit."

"Well, the rest of 'em, they just buy it from me. Cheaper than a ABC store. Same with the pot. Same with the pills."

"How about cable?" I said. "Does everyone get cable television?"

"Most do."

"And internet?"

"Yeah, sure, through the cable. We set up a couple hot spots, you know? For cell phones."

I said, "You're the boss here. Is it okay with you if I take a few laps before I go? Drive around and make notes?"

"Sure, sure, anyone working for Wayne and Mr. Summers can do what they want, I reckon. Ain't you gonna call Wayne?"

I looked at my watch. "He's at least ten minutes gone by now. I hate to call him all the way back, waste half an hour of his time."

"Yeah. Yeah, okay."

"I'll return as soon as I can. Poke my head in and see his supply unit."

"You know," he said, and he scratched at his thigh. "You want, I can let you in now. I got the key."

"Keith, that would be great. You'd save me a couple hours. Like I said, Wayne told me you were handy."

Keith's face broke into an eager-to-please smile. He dug into his pocket and limped to the unit. He used separate keys for the two locks. Opened the door and punched in a three-number sequence to disarm the system. Flipped a switch.

"Here you go," he said.

The unit had been stripped of all interior framework. It was a small warehouse, essentially, which smelled of mold. One corner was piled with necessaries like toilet paper and cleaner. Another corner with jugs of moonshine. A third with cellophane packages. Marijuana.

"Okay." I nodded. "Pretty simple operation."

"Yeah, simple. Keeps everyone quiet."

"Ever have thieves try to break in?"

"Sure, now and then. Alarm goes off and all the tenants release the dogs." He grinned and his face turned a little red. "Bastards only try it once."

"Wayne makes the moonshine himself," I said. "What about the pot, do you know? They grow it locally?"

"Sure." The grin on his face remained strong. "All that farmland, what else you gonna do with it?"

"Good question, Keith."

"Grow pot!"

"Milk, moonshine, and marijuana," I said.

"That's what Franklin County is all about. Cows and liquor and gettin' high."

"And guns," I said. "Don't forget guns."

"Yeah. Well. Folks here don't much have call for guns. Wayne don't bring 'em and sometimes it's hard for people like us to get them. We could. But got better things to do with money."

"Do you worry about the police? Not much of this unit is legal."

"Naw, police usually don't care. We're a quiet group else Wayne makes us leave. And if we leave, got nowhere to go. We don't bother police so they don't bother us. Right?"

"Keith, you've been tremendously helpful."

13

Kix and I spent the morning at a playground off the greenway. He zipped down all the slides, gazed condescendingly at kids with less impressive fathers, and relaxed in the stroller while I jogged laps. I took him to his sitter's house around lunch and his need for a nap was desperate.

Roxanne met me at the door. Laundry had exploded around her living room.

She accepted Kix and said, "Kristin called me."

"You old women, gossiping over your tea."

"Is that a quote?"

"Close to it."

She smiled and shook her head at me. "In a classroom, Mack August? You filthy private cop."

"Not that private, it turns out."

"So it's getting serious between you two," she said.

"She says she can separate the physical from the emotional. Her idea, not mine."

"Do you believe her?"

"I do not. The two seem intertwined, from my experience."

"What about the other girl?" she said. "The one you're not technically dating."

"She's still lovely."

"You're treading into dangerous waters, Mack."

"And yet you look thrilled. Perhaps it is you who are the monster."

"My world is laundry and dishes and diapers. I need this."

I turned to go. "I'll shoot your husband in the foot. Give you some
drama."

I MET Ronnie and Calvin Summers at her office. He was already
there, sitting on the corner of her desk, arms crossed. She stood when
I entered and my breath threatened to mutiny.

He wore slacks and a pale blue golf shirt. I wore a blue blazer,
mostly to hide my gun so Natasha the receptionist wouldn't swoon.

"All right, August. Report," he said.

"How about instead I return the remainder of your retainer and
with it you purchase some manners."

Ronnie sat down and her face paled.

He didn't speak. Remained perched, arms crossed. The muscle in
his jaw clenched as he thought.

I sat and smiled at Ronnie.

"Hello Mackenzie," she said.

"Hello Counselor."

"The fuck, August? You got a problem with me asking for
updates?" he said.

"I'm not your employee. I'm a consultant. You don't get to bark
demands at me. You didn't 'ask for an update.' You issued an order.
Do it again and you're on your own."

"Christ. Everyone's so sensitive."

I shrugged. "I'm an old-fashioned kinda girl."

"How the hell'd you get into Marcus Morgan's good graces? That
guy doesn't like anyone."

"The man's got suspect taste in friends."

Ronnie eyed me suspiciously. "Marcus Morgan? You work with Marcus Morgan? How do you know him?"

"I taught his son some manners. He respected it."

"Marcus Morgan has strong ties to the underworld," Ronnie said. "Are you aware?"

"Hey," Calvin said without looking her. "Attorney. We're using your office. Don't need your mouth. Keep it closed."

I held eye contact with her. "I am aware of who and what Marcus is. We don't work together. We're essentially wary acquaintances."

Calvin said, "So, August. How about I ask nicer so you can unclench. Provide me with an update *please*. How's that?"

"I'm making progress," I said. "But it's been tricky."

"Tricky? Tricky how?"

"You failed to convey crucial aspects of your operation. Unearthing them has required time and effort."

"Unearthing what?"

"You are a significant producer of moonshine and marijuana. Did you not believe that information germane to the task?"

"Marijuana?" Ronnie asked.

Calvin sniffed dismissively. "Didn't know if I could trust you, August, that's all."

"You're a drug dealer looking for an informant. Accept this professional advice free of charge: the informant probably works on the illegal side of your operation, not the legal."

"You're growing marijuana?" Ronnie asked her father. "How much?"

"Shut up."

Helpfully, I offered, "Truckloads."

"Dad." She stood. "Is that accurate?"

He didn't answer.

"Holy shit, Dad. You're producing and distributing a Schedule I narcotic. On top of the deferred tax evasion sentence, this would put you away forty years. Fines in the millions."

"Shut your fucking mouth."

"That amount is a felony, not a misdemeanor—"

He twisted on the desk and struck her across the mouth with his fingers. She gasped and tumbled backwards.

I came out of my seat so quickly Calvin nearly fell off his perch. He wasn't a small man but for this moment in time I eclipsed the rest of his universe.

"Summers," I said.

"August, the hell, back off!" A fearful waver crept into his voice, pitching it higher.

"I'm not stupid enough to stick my nose into the privileged affairs between an attorney and her client," I said. Our faces were separated by four inches. "Much less get in the way of family drama. And I don't presume I can fix problems because I'm male and that she can't because she's female. But if you hit her again I'm going to squeeze your hand until the bones break. You won't be able to stop me. It won't be chivalrous. Just simple rage."

He didn't say anything but his perfect hairline began to dampen with sweat.

I wanted to ask him if he understood but he obviously did.

I wanted to ask her if she was okay but she obviously wasn't. And it would demean her.

I sat back down, ignoring the dragon within, the animal hate that wanted to break his neck. I didn't look at Ronnie.

She got up and went to the small refrigerator in the corner. Got an ice cube, wrapped it in a paper towel, and held it to her mouth.

"What," Calvin said. "You think Marcus Morgan doesn't strike his child? For discipline?"

"Marcus has a son. Who is in tenth grade. And I would bet he strikes neither his son nor his wife," I said.

"I've seen Morgan kill people."

"Me too. But he respects his family."

"You've seen Marcus Morgan kill people?" Ronnie asked around the ice. She looked at both of us.

Her father didn't answer but he looked as though he wondered if his silence would anger me.

"I have," I said.

"Big Shot here has caught the attention of the Mafioso," Calvin said, indicating me with his chin. His voice still had a faint tremble. "Makes him think he's something he's not, maybe."

"Counselor Summers, what was the nature of the evidence presented by the prosecution?" I asked. "It must have been solid for Calvin to push for a plea deal."

"Accurate financial records," she said. Her lip had begun to swell.

"Does that not narrow down our list of suspects?"

"No," Calvin said. "No it doesn't. And believe it or not, that's my fault." He stood and released a frustrated sigh and looked out her window. "I fucked up. I sent some figures to my accountant, Tom Bradshaw. He told me you came by and made an ass of yourself. Anyway. I hit the wrong button. I hit reply all, instead of reply, that kind of thing. You know how it goes. I sent the files to everyone. Well, most everyone. Everyone who matters. And anyone who doesn't matter could have heard through gossip."

"The files you sent were unmistakably incriminating?" I asked.

"No, not unmistakably. The numbers were buried. Had to go looking for them. Some nosey motherfucker did."

"And there's no way to discover who opened the files?"

"Not that we know of," Ronnie said.

"I imagine everyone did, the ungrateful shits."

I said, "Okay. This helps. If you want me to continue, I want to see the email and I want the names of everyone. Not just the legal side."

"Got half a mind to fire your ass, August."

"Gasp."

"Then again, Marcus likes you. Duane likes you. They must see something I don't."

I asked, "What do you think, Counselor Summers? Should he fire my ass?"

"Considering the sensitive subject matter and your proven discretion, I see no reason for a change. Furthermore it would waste time."

"Get me the names. Of everyone."

"Apparently I don't have the entire list," she said.

"I'll get you the names, August. Give me half a day and I'll get you the names." He slid off Ronnie's desk and stalked out. "And you get me the fucking informant and get out of my hair."

The heavy door slammed after his exit.

Ronnie and I sat unspeaking for sixty seconds. Somehow both of us shared the same grief and embarrassment. As though we'd done something wrong.

"I'm not going to," I said at last, "but I'd like to rip your father's ears off."

She smiled and winced.

"Thank you. For not making that worse."

"One day when you've had enough and you decide to kick your old man's ass, I hope I'm there to see it."

"Do me a favor, Mackenzie. Please leave. I need a moment."

"Certainly."

"I wasn't joking, was I," she said. "That night in the parking lot when I told you I was a wreck, that I didn't deserve you."

"Your father doesn't deserve me, that's for damn sure." I stood and paused by her inner door. "You, on the other hand...wanna go to a baseball game with me tomorrow?"

"Yes, Mackenzie. Very much. I'll get someone to cover my shift at the bar."

I said, "You're still bartending."

"I am."

"Your father makes you."

She nodded and winced. "He does. But I enjoy it."

"It's a way he exerts control over you."

She changed subject, "Will Kix be at the game?"

"He will. I'll pick you up."

"It's a date," she said.

"Control your raging hormones. We're just friends."

"Affectionate friends."

"Manny will also be in attendance."

"Your roommate?" she asked. "The beautiful one?"

"In our household he ranks fourth."

"Tough competition. Close the door on your way out?"

She still had the ice pressed to her lower lip and water ran down her wrist. I winked and closed the door.

Natasha looked up from her desk and gave me a weak smile.

"You heard," I said.

"I heard everything."

"Does that happen often?"

"Let's just say...I hope you break his hand."

14

I picked Ronnie up from her apartment at the River House, a former industrial building modernized for residential millennialism, complete with climbing wall and bar. She wore shorts and an off-shoulder white tunic with a notch collar. I maintained my composure and opened the passenger door for her but instead she slid into the backseat and began playing with Kix.

Kix, the faint-hearted philanderer, did not maintain his composure. He reacted like it was Christmas morning.

"Oh, Mackenzie. He's so unbelievable gorgeous."

I drove toward Salem. "Don't get worked up. He performs thusly for all the hot girls."

"Just how many am I competing with?"

"Perhaps you should wear your engagement ring more often. You know, as a pneumonic device."

"Are you still dating that awful woman?"

"How do you know she's awful?" I said.

"A woman's intuition. She's awful."

"I detect a hint of jealousy."

"Hell yes you do."

"It looks good on you."

"She's awful. Trust me, I'm an attorney."

"Your reasoning is backwards," I observed. "And mendacious."

"Have you seen the awful woman today?"

"No."

"Texted her?"

"No," I said.

"She's not the one for you."

"You know this?"

She shrugged a shoulder, a motion I admired in the rearview. "I intuit it. I am perspicuous."

"What's a boy to do? All the good girls are taken."

"Kix doesn't care that I'm engaged. Why should you?"

"Kix is a slut."

"Mackenzie! No sir." She laughed, perhaps my favorite sound. Even the toddler stopped babbling to listen. "I object."

"A spade is a spade."

"What did you do today? Track down nefarious informants?"

"I visited with Mr. Stokes, the property manager. You know him, I believe," I said.

"I do."

"He might be your biggest fan."

"He's harmless. Better than most men," she said.

"And I poked my nose around the Calvin Summers marijuana plantation."

"Plantation? So it's more than just a few clay pots?"

"An entire field. Maybe more."

She closed her eyes and let her forehead rest on the side of Kix's car seat. He patted her cheek.

"An entire field," she said.

"Met a nice man named Ruben Collier. He nearly opened fire with his shotgun when I arrived but we hashed out the misunder-standing. He's giving me a thorough tour tomorrow."

She groaned softly.

"Hashed out," I prompted. "Get it?"

"Yes Mackenzie."

"I'm incredibly funny," I said. "And I'm positive Calvin Summers is not attached to the moonshine and marijuana operations in any legal or traceable way. Otherwise he'd be a fool, and he isn't. Criminally incompetent perhaps but not a fool. I'm going to probe deeper into his infrastructure."

"Mackenzie, I do not wish to pry into your methods. But. What will you do when you discover the informant's identity?"

"An insightful question."

"Because I know you. To some extent. You have a soft heart. And I'm curious what will happen if the informant has a family. Is just trying to make ends meet. What if the person is not 'nefarious'?"

"Let's you and I jump off that bridge together, if we come to it," I said.

She nodded to herself and her eyes were momentarily fixed on something far beyond my mirror. "Okay. If you need my input, I will jump with you."

We arrived in Salem after the first pitch had been thrown. My son couldn't stomach all nine innings so we usually came late and left early. And my old man couldn't stomach sitting in the stands with the hoi polloi so he'd rented a private box. This was the Salem Red Sox's second game of the season and the night was warm. The heaters in our box were turned off.

Timothy August sat in the front row of the balcony with Sheriff Stackhouse. They'd both come straight from work, wearing white button-up shirts with the collar loosened. Each held a beer, that necessary nectar of America's pastime.

Ronnie sat in the chair behind the sheriff and gave her a friendly hug around the shoulders. "Hello beautiful."

"Veronica Summers, hey babe. It actually hurts to look at you. I was young and nubile once. My Lord, look at those legs."

"One must dress up for the August household. Have you ever seen such a collection of perfect masculinity?"

"I'd marry any one of them," Stackhouse said. "But at the moment I choose the one most experienced."

"I'll happily take the leftovers."

Manny observed, "These white women, so...what's the word?"

"Prurient," I said.

"That is not it."

"Lubricious?"

"No. Horny, is what I thought."

Stackhouse patted Manny's knee and said, "Even better."

Ronnie held Kix on her lap and fed him dry cereal throughout innings two through five. Manny and I engaged in highly suspect scorekeeping, scrutinizing each other's sheets for unforgivable errors. Stackhouse and Timothy August held hands and chatted affectionately and in general displayed a disgusting amount of friendliness. Hot dogs were consumed by all. Our attendant, a student at Roanoke College by the looks of her, waited breathlessly on Manny and kept his cup full. Every so often, reluctantly, she filled ours too.

The Sox hit a home run in the fifth and Ronnie asked, "Is he good?"

"That's Andrew Benintendi," I said. "He'll play in the majors soon."

"I like the way he looks in his uniform."

"Only because you haven't seen a real man wear one."

"I'll buy you the outfit if you promise to model it for me. Privately."

Timothy August sighed. "Ah yes, this is the type of conversation a father dreams of overhearing."

"Could be worse," Manny said. "Could be a señorita who isn't Ronnie."

"Thank you, Manny," she said. "I'll buy you an outfit too."

"I'm inspecting a marijuana field tomorrow," I said. "Want to go?"

"Sí. Donde?" Manny said.

"I'll drive. But it's conditional on you not arresting or shooting anyone."

"Que?"

"Because we're playing nice."

"Sounds like a bunch of old women knitting. But I'll go."

"I'll go too," Stackhouse said over her shoulder.

"The invitation was not extended to you, copper. This is outside your jurisdiction."

"An entire field?" she asked.

"Glorious, no?"

"I'd get my name in the papers for bringing in that much."

"You're a noble-hearted public servant, no doubt. But ultimately not invited."

"I'll follow you."

"Oh dear," I said. "Whatever shall I do."

She grinned and twisted in her seat to get a better look at me. "You think you can shake my tail?"

"I could shake you in a phone booth."

"What are you working on? This is juicy," she said.

Ronnie shifted in her chair and remained silent.

"Privileged information, Sheriff," I told her.

"Big Mack here got himself in thick with the Mafioso," Manny said.

Now it was my father's turn to twist backwards. "The Mafioso? Perhaps further explanation is in order."

"Oh great. You told on me to my dad," I said.

"Lo siento."

Timothy asked, "What exactly is the Mafioso?"

"The criminal underworld. It has many names. I'm not involved. A brief entanglement only."

"The entanglement is concluded?" Timothy asked.

"I plead the Fifth."

Ronnie nodded approval.

"Son."

"It will be concluded forthwith," I told him.

"Powerful people?" he asked.

Manny nodded. "Muy ponderoso. But maybe not as badass as Mack."

Dad glanced at Stackhouse, who shrugged, and then he scrutinized Manny. "I'm his father. I worry. Should I be worried?"

"Mack ain't as feeble as he look."

"You'll help? If he needs it?"

I frowned. "Help? Who needs help?"

"Sí, Señor August. He's Tonto and I'm...the other one."

"The Lone Ranger," I said. "And you've got it backwards."

Manny threw his hand into the air. "White people. So racist."

In the sixth inning, my perfect evening was marred by the discovery of Kristin Payne in the stands. Kristin Payne the Roanoke College professor, athletic coach, and sexual predator. She sat with a pack of friends throwing peanuts and laughing. Our luxury box was level with her seat.

She'd seen me. That was apparent. Because soon after I spotted her we made eye contact. I smiled. She responded with her best effort and she waved and returned to the game.

Next to me, Kix bounced happily on the lap of the blonde long-legged sun goddess. Whom Kristin also would have observed.

Luckily for me Kristin could separate the physical from the emotional. Or so she claimed.

Ugh.

It was going to end badly.

It always ended badly.

This was why you didn't let college professors give you lap dances in their classroom. Everyone knew that.

15

Manny and I met Ruben Collier on a rutted nondescript dirt road in Franklin County. A chilly wind had blown in to remind us that early April wasn't always daffodils and sunshine but Ruben didn't seem to mind. He was a bald friendly black man, strong hands, large eyes and shiny dome. He'd dressed in heavy boots and a thick fleece-lined jacket that zipped to his chin, much warmer than Manny and me; we stamped and shivered as he led us deeper into the budding forest.

"We're walking," Manny observed, intelligently. "Why do we walk?"

"On account of that toy car of yours wouldn't make it," Ruben responded. "Only four-wheel drive trucks up here."

"Do you worry about police?" I asked. I ignored the crack about a toy car because I was impervious to verbal insults. And also complaining would make me look even more childish than my toy Honda.

"Naw. There's ten thousand dirt roads like this within twenty miles. Them good ol' deputies don't care. Hell, half of them smoke up. Maybe all of them."

"I miss smoking la mota," Manny said.

"Why you quit?"

"The white guy. He's got principles."

"You fellas gay?" Ruben asked.

"He wishes," I said.

"Not that it matters none."

"I was gay, I'd pick someone snores less," Manny said.

Ruben led us through a ten-foot high chicken-wire fence (used to prevent deer from getting high) to the field I'd glimpsed yesterday. I'd only glimpsed it because of Ruben's shotgun. He'd called Summers and then told me I'd get the tour tomorrow. The field was a mile off the road and a little anticlimactic. A mere plot of dirt with tender shoots stretching in infancy. Not sure what I expected. But something other than a couple acres of tilled farmland. This didn't strike me as sinister.

"Ain't she beautiful." Ruben grinned and stretched both arms wide.

"I thought marijuana was usually grown in a greenhouse," I said.

"Can be. But that's when folks worried about being seen. Don't worry that here. Here, I do it right. I prep the soil. Turn the dirt with lime. Sow with a good auto flowering strain and keep'em moist. Cover this whole patch with a tarp, a frost comes."

"Is Virginia a good climate for growing pot?"

"Not the best. It's fine. Can't use some of the nicer strains. Wish I could use a nice haze seed to get better yield but they won't hold up."

"You're a pro," I said.

He accepted this with a royal nod.

"How much money will this crop make?" I asked.

"This patch pays my bills for the year. Got another patch puts my kids through college. Got a third smaller field sends me and the wife to Hawaii each winter."

"Is Calvin Summers the owner?"

He grinned. "Gets tricky. Farmer owns the land. Somebody rents it. Somebody else hires me. Somebody else moves it. All under the table. I don't ask no questions. But Mr. Summers, he the chief."

"And Wayne Cross?"

"Wayne comes take his cut. He gets the leftovers. Cheap stuff, couple seasons old I keep stored."

"He doesn't get the good stuff."

"No sir, good stuff goes somewhere else. Don't know where. Ain't my job. Be my educated guess, though, Mr. Summers don't do much distributing. Man don't much like getting his hands dirty."

Manny nodded. He hated dirt. Wouldn't even help with my flower beds.

I turned in a circle, examining where I stood. In a literal sense. It was as though we were on a different continent, far removed from Roanoke city. It only took sixty minutes driving to reach Ruben but it felt like another time zone. I was out of my element. Didn't know what questions to ask the man.

"Do you help with the moonshine stills?" I asked.

"No sir. I'm a farmer. Don't know about liquor."

"Calvin Summers was incarcerated. You knew about that?"

"Sure. We all did." He crouched and began rearranging the dirt around a few of the green saplings.

"I'm a consultant, hired to improve his enterprise. What would your suggestion be?"

"My suggestion? Not a learned enough man for that."

"That's—"

"But if I did have an opinion on it, I'd say there's one too many hands stirring the soup."

"What do you mean?" I asked.

He stopped smoothing the dirt. Didn't look up. "Summers is a man who don't micromanage. Sets up the system, trusts his people, likes seeing the money come in. But maybe some people shouldn't be trusted. He's got the farmer, he's got me, he's got wholesale buyers and movers, he's got Wayne, and all the other stuff he's got. Just lets us work. You know how much oversight I got? None. Easy to skim. Easy to keep extra profit. I don't. You understand me, I don't. But it gets mighty tempting. Maybe some people don't fight the temptation."

"Zero oversight."

"None, no sir."

"Hombres in Los Angeles," Manny said. "The guys moving money and drugs and guns and girls, they got safety measures. Triple checks. You skim? They know and they kill your kid."

"That's right. Triple checks? Mr. Summers don't have double checks. Or any safety measures. He too rich to care if a shipment makes ten grand or eight," Ruben said.

"Too rich or too stupid."

He grinned at Manny. "Well. You said it. Not me."

"So people steal from Calvin," I said.

"My guess? Lotta people do."

"He has a dairy farm. But doesn't care about it. Calvin never visits, never inspects it. He pays the bills, the milk gets made, milk gets bought, and he gets a check at the end of the month. He sees a profit, he's happy," I said.

"Yes. That's it. Same with the marijuana. He gets money. Stays in his fancy house, stays in his fancy car and fancy suits, doesn't worry. Lets me do my work. Lets folk steal."

"You think Calvin knows? That people steal?"

Ruben said, "Would guess so. Comes with the territory. He knew how much, though? He wouldn't like it."

Ruben was thorough. I scrutinized the surrounding forest but couldn't see any trapping of farm work. No toolshed. No tractors. No bags of fertilizer. The man was fastidious.

I asked, "Do you know Boyd Hunt? The dairy farmer?"

"I know Boyd. Good man. Man doesn't skim."

I nodded. "That's my impression too."

"His wife, on the other hand?" Ruben shook his head. "Angry woman. Angry at her husband, angry at Mr. Summers for buying their farm. Not so sure about Mrs. Hunt."

Manny was examining the bottom of his shoes, eying the mud with distaste. "I like Señora Hunt. Anger is good."

"How much of your last harvest did you move?" I asked.

"Nearly all. Say, ninety percent is gone. Wayne will get most what I got left next few months, before this crop's ready."

"You keep last year's remainder here, on the premises?"

"Yes sir. Got it insulated below ground. Animals can't get at it. Most folks who don't buy it fresh don't care about the oils drying out. The buyers who care, they buy it freshly cured. I pack it in jars for them. Keep it out the sunlight till they pick it up."

I asked, "Do you know anyone who doesn't like Calvin?"

"No, everybody likes Mr. Summers. Who don't like a boss keeps his nose out your business? Mr. Summers set up a system that keeps us fed. He don't hassle us and he don't care if we steal."

"We?" I said.

"Well." He winked. "Not me. Don't bite the hand that feeds you."

Manny shot me a knowing look. "Good advice, you ask me, amigo."

MANNY and I returned to my toy Honda and made it half a mile before two squad cars fell in behind us and hit their lights.

"What a strange coincidence," I said.

"Must be a mistake. Because there's no way the local fuzz would be upset with you. You, such a pleasant gringo."

I pulled over on a particularly desolate stretch of country road. Turned on my phone's microphone and slipped it into the pocket on the chest of my jacket. A deputy stepped out of each car and approached on either side of mine. I buzzed down the window.

The man on my side, a younger guy, barely old enough to shave, said, "License and registration."

I complied.

Deputy on the other side knocked on Manny's window. He lowered it.

"Hola."

The deputy didn't respond immediately. He was older and heavy-set. Pot belly and thick neck. His shirt was placing a staggering amount of pressure on the buttons.

"Hablas ingles?" Manny said.

"What I want to know is," the heavy deputy drawled, "what a fucking spic and a nosey cop for hire are doing out here in God's country?"

"We're gay," I said. "Moving in pronto and bringing all our gay with us."

The heavy guy stepped back. "Out of the car. *Pronto*."

Manny glanced my way. "We playing nice?"

"At least for another minute."

We got out. They arranged us side by side, hands on the roof of my car. They stood behind us. "Don't be jealous," I said. "I have to do a lot of squats to look this good in jeans."

No response.

I said, "Something wrong, deputies?"

"Yeah. Something's wrong. Saw you here the other day, faggot. And seen you around Happy Hills." It sounded like he was wrestling to keep his belt up, the poor thing. "And I want to know why."

"Sightseeing," I said. "I'm enjoying the farmland and Appalachian rot."

"Not what I heard."

"What'd you hear?" I asked.

"Heard you're looking into things you shouldn't be. Couple'a queers should mind your business."

"You strike me as a man who's best buddies with Wayne Cross. Am I right? I'm totally right."

"Don't matter. What matters is you stay away. You get me?"

"Stay away from what?"

"From here. Stop trying to be smart."

"Stay off this road?" I said. "What's wrong with this road?"

"This road ain't for you."

"I like this road. I'm definitely coming back here, to this road," I said.

"You are."

"I am. How'd you know where to find us?"

"I know. I know everything," he said.

"Oh yeah? How do you spell cognitive dissonance?"

"Think twice about your mouth, boy. Gonna get you in trouble. You think I can't run you over? You think I can't tie you down and run you over with your own fucking car?"

In the window's reflection, I saw him remove the nightstick from his belt.

"Uh-oh," I said. "Think twice, Mr. Fat Officer, before doing something stupid. Feel my muscles first. They're enormous. And there's two of us, only one of you."

"You blind, queer? Two of us. And we're the law."

"Yeah, but your young friend won't join in. He's too young. Not used to confrontation yet," I said. "Not angry enough."

"Smart-ass, a beating'd be good you, fucking faggot."

"Oye, policia," Manny said. "He was joking. About the gay thing. Go easy, amigo, else I floss your teeth with the nightstick."

"Before we visit violence upon your corpulent body, Deputy, mind telling us who sent you?" I asked.

Poor Fat Officer had enough. He cracked Manny in the temple with the stick. Or he tried to, at least. Manny raised his arm and caught it inside his fist, near his ear. He twisted and brought the deputy crashing into the side of my Honda, hard enough to break the man's ribs. The deputy slid to the ground.

I turned and gathered the collar of the younger deputy. Held him close. "Relax. All right? Don't do anything stupid. He got you into this and now he's paying for it."

The kid's eyes were wild. Didn't know what to do. Deputy sheriffs shouldn't let two guys like us boss him around, right? Should he be a hero?

I said, "I'm former Los Angeles police. Manny there is a US marshal in Roanoke. Just relax."

Manny slapped Fat Officer hard across the mouth. "Hit me with a stick? Hit me with a stick, pendejo?" Manny pulled out his pistol and pressed the barrel firmly up the man's nostril. "Call me a few more names."

I asked the young deputy, "Who told you to rough us up?"

The kid's voice squeaked. "I...I don't know. Yopp told me to follow his lead. Said we needed to run off a couple'a troublemakers."

Yopp got his head kicked by Manny. His skull rebounded off my tire.

"Manny," I said. "I think your point has been made."

"Maybe," Manny said. He delivered another kick, this one to the man's ear. Manny's chest was rising with deep breaths. "I get mad. Muy loco, amigo."

"I know. But he's bleeding from his ears and nose. We're good."

Manny walked away, his boots crunching on gravel, to remove himself from temptation.

"Hey. Yopp. You hear me? Who told you about us?" I called.

Yopp groaned. Uselessly.

I asked the kid, "You know Wayne Cross?"

"Sure." He swallowed, his Adam's apple bobbing. "Sure, I know Wayne."

"You're wondering what happens now," I said. "I got an idea. Nothing happens now. I recorded this encounter. I got Yopp cursing at us and telling us we needed an ass beating. He won't report us because he'll get fired. So you don't report us either because you watched your friend get smacked around. An officer of the law doing nothing? No good. Don't let anyone see the camera footage from your car. This goes away. Yopp learns a lesson. Right?"

The kid gulped again. I released him.

"Yopp had this coming," I said.

"Yeah. Yeah he did."

"Yopp gives you any trouble, punch him in the nose. He'll learn quick. Right?"

"Yeah." The kid laughed uneasily. "Yeah, okay."

"Manny? You know why I'm the Lone Ranger and you're not? I drive. Let's go."

16

I sat in my office, sneakers crossed on the desk, bouncing a Nerf ball off the window. The windows had been installed sometime during the Roman empire and the pane rattled threateningly. My coffee had gone cold and the last piece of bacon beckoned from my desk but so far I'd abstained. Bacon got even better the more you wanted it. My fantasy baseball stats were displayed prominently on the screen of my laptop and '90s alternative music came from the bluetooth speaker. Green Day at the moment.

I knew the Franklin County sheriff was a straight-laced man, ran things by the book, heart of gold, yada yada. He hadn't sent Yopp on the sordid errand. Yopp had acted as an independent agent, trying to intimidate us because someone had tipped him off that he should. Perhaps Ruben Collier and his fields of weed? I doubted it. Weed might be the impetus but Ruben wouldn't have been the one to call for the backup — didn't strike me as the type. Someone else was worried about us and it wasn't Calvin.

Probably Wayne, that bastion of nobility. He'd either spotted me or heard about my snooping.

Didn't mean he was Calvin's informant, though. The man could simply hate me. Or worry I would wreck his source of income.

My eyes fell to the list of names provided by Calvin. I had a few more to visit and then the real work began. I would pick a couple of the feeble-hearted and falsely inform them I knew they were the informant. Tell them that Calvin knew and he was furious. Rattle them and see what fell out. Either I was right or I was wrong, and if I was wrong then they might admit truths which would help me. Not exactly a virtuous method but it was tried and effective.

I didn't want to do it yet, however. I was tired of Franklin County drives and needed a day off.

Perhaps I should visit Ronnie. And her couch.

No sir, to borrow her phrase. No sir, you're dating Kristin Payne. Right?

Kristin.

I kept forgetting her.

I should probably invite her over. We hadn't communicated since the ball game.

I texted her. Ever the gentleman.

Come over. Pick a night. I'll cook.

No immediate response. So she wasn't sitting around, bouncing a ball across her room and waiting on my text. Girls are weird.

The stairs squeaked and Clay Fleming came into my office. Clay Fleming, guy from Floyd. We'd played poker together. He was dressed in work boots, khakis, and a jean jacket, dirt stains ubiquitous.

I stood and shook his hand, which was rough-hewn and strong. A wedding band glinted on his left. I said, "Clay Fleming. You're the redneck."

"Redneck and damn proud of it. So you're a true private detective with a true private detective office, just like Humphrey Bogart in those black and white movies."

"Philip Marlowe. He was the best. And I, a mere simulacrum."

"A mere simulacrum," he said, sitting in one of my client chairs. "Whatever the hell that means. You need to get one of them doors with the glass, so the girl's silhouette is visible through it. You know?"

"The femme fatale."

"That's the one, damsel in distress, big boobs hanging out, help me, Mack, I'm in trouble."

"You'd be surprised how often that doesn't happen."

"Still. Probably better-looking girls than the heifers I hang out with." He pointed at his mud-caked boots.

"But perhaps we deal with the same amount of crap," I said. "Yours happens to be literal."

"I like this office. Got a good feel to it. You're a baseball fan." He threw his hand toward my shelves.

"I am, but Bryce Harper leaves for the Yankees and it'll test my mettle."

"You even got a bible sitting over there," he said. "You read that thing?"

"I do."

"Used to go to church with my grandmother when I was a boy. Floyd Baptist. You a religious man?"

"I am not. Religion strikes me as a sort of rule-following to appease the powers that be. I'm not so great at following rules."

"Then why read it?"

"I believe the documents within contain truth. Doesn't mean I understand it, I must confess. But I'm desperate for truth. Most days I stare, hoping wisdom will impart itself. You know Jesus tells us to love our enemies?"

"He does?" Clay asked.

"Indeed."

"The hell is that about?"

"Strikes me as the kind of thing God would say. Now I just gotta figure out why."

"You ever worry at night, when all is quiet and you're falling asleep, about maybe you've got life all wrong? That you been aiming at stuff don't matter?" he asked, staring at my desk and at the universe beyond.

"That's precisely why I read the book."

"You figure it all out, you let me know," he said. "So how's it coming, the Calvin Summers thing? Got some of us antsy, Calvin getting snitched on. Could happen to us, you know."

"Slow and tedious work. Thus far no one has volunteered to take the fall," I said.

"Don't blame them. Whoever it is, he's getting the shit kicked out of him and then shot," Clay said.

"Think so?"

"Has to be. Snitches don't get stitches, Mack, snitches get made an example. Look what happens, Calvin will say. Look what happens, you send me to prison."

I liked Clay's manner of speaking. It was without affect, straightforward. Kinda slow and polite, a twinge of the country accent on the vowels.

"Clay, you don't strike me as the kinda guy to kick the shit out of someone and then shoot them," I said. "You want coffee?"

"Thank you, no. Already had three cups. And you're right, I ain't the type. But I ain't in the same work as the other guys."

"What work are you in?"

"I raise beef cattle," he said.

"Sure, Marcus Morgan likes to play cards with beef farmers. Makes sense."

He grinned. "And I got a moonshine business."

"Same as Calvin?"

"Summers is more diversified as me. As you're probably discovering. But me? All I do is hooch."

"Any money in it?" I asked.

"I run shine all over this part of the state. And parts of North Carolina, West Virginia, and Kentucky. Hell yeah there's money."

"You don't deal with wholesalers?"

"Naw, I like to sell directly to a handful of distributors," he said. "Me or one of my boys."

"Enlighten me," I said. "I'm a simple pure-minded suburban episcopal. Seems to me like half of Franklin County brews their own shine. I don't even know if brew is the right word. But it's everywhere. How do you make money?"

"So yesterday I take a truck north up Interstate 81. Right? Got the truck loaded with strawberry shine. Little too sweet but it'll do. I sell fifty jars for forty bucks a piece in Lexington. Fifty in Lynchburg. A hundred in Harrisonburg. And so on. Mostly to guys who got the taste but not enough time to make their own. They collect money from friends and meet me in the parking lot, or maybe they give them out as gifts, shit, I don't care. I get home last night, I've sold five hundred jars."

"Forty a piece, that's twenty thousand dollars," I said, hoping he'd notice my keen math skills.

"Twenty thousand dollars. After expenses, like materials and equipment and couple guys work with me, I keep about five bucks a jar. So yesterday I made twenty-five hundred. I'll do it again next week, heading south. And then again, week after. So for me, Mack, I clear over ten grand a month. No taxes, just clean cold cash. And that's on top of the beef."

I laced my fingers over my stomach and leaned back in my chair. "Ten grand a month's pretty good."

"Ten grand in pure profit. That ain't income, that's after expenses. Guy in Floyd, like me, who already owns a cattle ranch, getting ten grand on top? I'll retire at fifty-five with all I'll ever need, me and my kids."

"Lucky for me, virtue is its own reward. I'll retire and live off all that goodwill."

"Hah. Keep dreaming, partner."

"Why are you telling me this?" I asked. "If it's purely for my company, I understand. Lesser men and women than you have fallen prey to my appeal."

"So. Listen, Mack. This has got to be off the record. Good?"

"No promises."

"No promises?" he said.

"I'll do my best. Won't repeat unless I have to. But you should know it up front."

"Yeah, well, Marcus trusts you. So listen. I produce and run shine.

And it's illegal. But I do it the right way. I'm a good man and I got a good business and I treat people right," Clay said.

"So you're an honest criminal," I said.

"That's right."

I took a guess. "And Calvin isn't?"

"Calvin's okay. He's into a lot. Lets others handle it for him. It's not Calvin who worries me."

I took another guess. "It's Wayne."

"It's Wayne. Got me spooked. Wayne's got aspirations. Wants to be a bigger player."

"But he's too stupid?"

"Not that he's too stupid but that he's too mean. And stupid. Our business, you don't be mean unless you got to. No contracts in our world, no paperwork. Odd as it sounds it's a gentleman's world. You met Edgar Knight at poker? Edgar wants moonshine, which he does sometimes, then I take him at his word. A handshake. Treats me right, I treat him right. I haul weapons for him sometimes. Same with Marcus. Same with Calvin. But Wayne? Wayne's a son of a bitch."

"Why's it seem like son of a bitches always trick big trucks?"

"Gotta disagree with you. I heard you at poker, joking about the mess in Franklin County. The broken Appalachian influence. And I can't argue about some of it. But guys like me, I ain't like that. I work from five in the morning until eight at night. And I drive a big-ass truck. So do most in Franklin and Floyd. To most of us it's all about the paycheck. You pay your own way, you're good by me. We work hard, take care of ourselves, take care of each other. It's the got'damn freeloaders I got a problem with. Live off government. Get their cousins pregnant. And them boys don't drive big-ass trucks. Can't afford 'em. They drive rust buckets."

"I apologize for my offensive comments. The result of ignorance and bias."

He waved it off. "See, this is the trouble with Wayne. He works for the paycheck but he don't help take care of his people. Don't care about the community. Me, I'm a gentleman. Folks work with me.

Wayne ain't a gentleman. And soon Calvin's gonna lose business. Start creating problems for us."

"Who is us?"

"Calvin and me. Marcus don't care. Edgar don't care, because they aren't country. Ain't from around here. But I don't like seeing generations of idiots falling down the same hole. And Wayne profits off it."

"The same hole? Something other than moonshine and marijuana, I presume."

"You're right. I don't mind the weed. And Franklin and Floyd don't have much blow. It's the prescription pills what kills us."

"Opioids. Hydrocodone. Oxycontin."

"That's right," he said."

"Is Calvin involved with pills?"

"Naw. It's Wayne. Pays off the docs or nurses or someone."

"Why not tell Calvin?" I asked. "About the usurper within his ranks?"

"Like I said, it's a gentleman's world. We tend not to meddle. I've hinted to Calvin and it didn't go over well."

"Could Wayne be the informant?"

He shook his head. "Naw. Not Wayne's style. Tattling to the feds, you kidding me? His hands are too dirty."

"Shame. I hate the guy."

"Loving your enemies is easier in theory than in practice, eh, Mack?"

"Truer words have never been spoken. I might get 'Easier Said than Done' etched on my tombstone."

17

The FBI had a small office in Roanoke off Kirk Street. This section of Kirk was paved brick and narrow and had an old-world charm. I parked and walked haplessly in circles looking for the entrance until a nondescript door opened and Jamie Patton stuck his head out.

"Mackenzie August?"

"Oh thank goodness. I was lost and on the verge of sheepishness," I said.

Jamie held the door for me. He looked early thirties, trim with broad shoulders, thinning brown hair. He had a friendly open face, wore a shirt and tie, pinstriped slacks and shiny black shoes. "Yeah, we're hard to find."

"Fidelity, bravery, and hidden doors."

"We're spooks and we can't feel smug if we advertise with big signs and windows," he said. Inside, he unlocked a heavy door using his handprint and we stepped into a security chamber. The door closed behind us and he unlocked the interior door with a retinal scanner and we emerged into a standard office hallway. Thin carpet. Five cubicles with sound-absorbing walls. Calendars hanging limply from pushpins. Someone was clicking quietly on a keyboard in the corner.

"Hallway is kind of a letdown after the secret entrance chamber of magic," I said.

"I know. We need machine-gun nests in here or something," he said.

"Thanks for meeting with me."

"Sure. Your boy Manny Martinez and I had lunch last week. He put in a good word. And Sheriff Stackhouse asked me to meet with you as a favor." He sat behind his laptop and indicated I take the other chair. His tiny space was cramped but neat and clean.

"It's wise to stay in her good graces," I said.

"I'd scale Everest if she asked. She's like a movie star, in my book. So, Mr. August, based on our brief phone conversation I've taken the liberty of accessing Calvin Summers's email."

I said, "Goodness you're quick. And way outside the law."

"None of this ever happened, you understand. But I assumed it would speed things up if I broke in."

"How'd you do that? You computer hackers strike me as sorcerers."

He shrugged and held out his hand, palm up. "I asked him his password and he told me."

"Liar."

"Well, that's the short version. Essentially I sent him a message which looked like official Gmail correspondence and he entered his password into the box. Presto. The man is not technologically savvy."

"He's not the sharpest criminal overlord either. Did you find anything I can use?"

He shook his head and leaned backwards so I could see the screen. "Afraid not. Certainly nothing which would hold up in court. Illegal seizure, that kind of thing."

"Technically I'm not after incriminating evidence. I want to know who opened that email he sent accidentally."

"I found it. Didn't take long. Calvin Summers doesn't use email much. He sends notes to his daughter and to his accountant. Sends the occasional Happy Birthday email. That's it. But there's no way to see who opened that email. I checked. I would have had to track it real time or attach a read receipt request. He received a couple replies but that's all we know for sure. A Mr. Stokes replied. So did Mr. Moss, who I believe operates his restaurant. They had nothing important to say. Can I ask what this is about?"

"I'm doing a job for him. Essentially trying to find out who betrayed him," I said. "Sounds fishy, I know. But I took the job with the intention of ultimately protecting the identity of the government's informant."

"So you're going to stab a mobster in the back," Jamie said.

"Figuratively, yes."

"I will bring flowers to your funeral."

"Fret not. As I said, he's not criminally proficient. He's more of an investment mobster," I said.

"Sorry I can't be more help. The easiest way to discover your Judas would be to hack the email of each recipient, but that would require a lot of time and effort and I cannot justify it."

"Wouldn't ask you to. I knew this was a long shot."

He said things about computers and the dark net which I didn't understand. In fact he filled an entire five minutes with esoteric nerd jargon, ultimately culminating with the fact that he couldn't help me. He leaned back in his swivel chair and laced his hands over his flat stomach. "What will you do now?"

"Pester suspects."

"That's essentially what I do for the FBI."

"We're a one-trick pony, what it boils down to," I said.

"You're a large man. I'd hate to be the one being pestered."

"Muscular. That's the word you're looking for. Not large."

"I'm curious how this job of yours resolves itself. I'll follow it with interest," Jamie said and he stood up to let me out through the portal of techno terror.

"Just ask. Don't hack into my phone."

"Ah. How boring."

18

Kristin Payne came over for dinner. She arrived barefoot, wearing short black shorts and a Lucky Brand pale blue tank top. She had the calves and quads of an athlete and she knew it. It was ten degrees too cool for her outfit but looking good is never easy.

I sprinkled salt and pepper onto our steaks while she drank a beer and bemoaned her academic responsibilities over the summer.

"And I don't think it matters how much work I take on," she was telling me. "I want to be a professor, I'll have to switch colleges."

"Being a professor is like getting tenure?"

"Yes, though it varies by institution. Point is you gotta get lucky and pay your dues, both. Can't just fuck your way to the top."

Kix sat in the high chair, watching her curiously over his cup of juice.

"Remember her sage advice, son. It's a lesson we can't learn soon enough," I said.

He requested more bananas. I acquiesced and then put our steaks onto the grill. I came back and chopped boiled potatoes.

Kix threw the cup at Kristin. It landed on the floor.

"Your kid dropped his thing," she said.

"I noticed. He's playing hard to get."

Manny came home. Said "Hola" to us both and went upstairs to change.

"Good God," she said, staring at the staircase. "Who the hell is that?"

"My roommate."

"He's gay?"

"He is not. Though he does sleep in my room," I said.

"Why?"

"Because even straight dudes are drawn to me."

"What?"

"Nothing. His sleeping arrangement is a long story. Full of violence and woe."

Kix started babbling at us.

"What's he want?" she asked.

"To be known."

"How do you make him stop?"

"I've never wondered. Or tried."

"I'm going to be the worst parent. If I have kids they'll be so screwed up," she said. Her beer was half gone and she swirled the thick liquid at the bottom of the glass.

"You? With your fancy human behavior degree?"

"I studied human behavior. Doesn't mean I'm a good one."

"How do you like your steak?" I asked.

"Medium well."

"Yikes. You are a bad one."

"Are you still working on the case with the abusive father?"

"I am and I've avoided tearing his ears off. Thanks for the advice."

"You're welcome. What kind of case is it, anyway?" she asked. She tipped her head back and consumed the rest of her beer. Set it down on the table with a thunk.

"I'm searching for someone."

"A missing person?"

"More of a hidden identity. Think of it like the board game Clue. The killer isn't missing, we just don't know who it is," I said.

"Oooo, is there a Miss Scarlet?"

"Indeed, and even a Colonel Mustard."

She started drawing lines on the table with condensation from the beer glass. Kix watched, confused why she didn't pay more attention to him. "How do you discover the killer?"

"I aggravate people and investigate relationships."

"That's it?"

"Everything is connected. The mystery person has hidden his or her tracks with painstaking care but it's impossible to erase all connections. Eventually I'll stumble over one."

"Like how," she said.

"Maybe a husband covering for his wife will slip up and he'll say the wrong thing. Maybe when I get close to the truth someone will start to get mad and defensive. It's hard to predict how the truth will surface. But surface it shall."

Manny went out for dinner and Kristin gaped unabashedly after him. She and I ate steaks and potatoes and salad, and I put Kix to bed. I came back and she had two beers out of the fridge. She gave me one and we sat on the leather couch in the front room of the house. Through the windows we could see a cool rain had begun falling, turning the lawn to winking crystal beneath streetlights.

She said, "I like your digs. Tall ceilings. Good woodwork." Her legs were tucked under her and she sat tall and erect.

"Someone told me it smells like cologne and masculinity and leather."

"Someone has an overactive imagination. Should we begin undressing?"

"Manny won't be gone long. And my old man is due soon. They come through that door sometimes and I'm positive they'd approve of your nakedness."

"And you?"

"I'm doing my best to avoid intimate congress," I said.

"You said this before. In the car. Is it a religious thing?"

"More like a survival thing."

Her face was close to mine and her eyes were narrow and piercing. "You don't want my body."

"Of course I do. But it'd be better if I didn't partake."

"Better for who?"

"Both of us, I imagine. Certainly for me," I said. "To thine own self be true. That kind of thing."

"You cannot hide from yourself behind platitudes."

"It's no platitude. I'm not a moralist. I'm simply broken."

She asked, "But you feel the urge? I'm desirable?"

"Absolutely. I want you twice. But. Have you ever snorted cocaine?"

She reeled back. "Of course not."

"I have. It's great. Don't let the anti-drug commercials fool you. Cocaine is the best. Drugs aren't addictive because they're boring. I still want to snort blow. But I haven't in years."

Her lips screwed up in a wry smile. "In this analogy, I'm cocaine."

"No. Sex is cocaine. You're the hot coke dealer."

"With great tits?"

"Better than any coke dealer I ever saw."

She set her beer bottle down and took my hand in both of hers. "Yeah but with sex there's no crash."

"For me there is. I felt awful."

"Why? Your performance was exemplary, Mack."

"Goes without saying. A sensational fifteen minutes."

"Fifteen minutes you wish. More like six."

"You were counting too fast," I courteously corrected her.

"Why the crash?"

"I think it's accumulated residue from old failed attempts at relationships. You're the one with the degree in human behavior, you tell me."

"How do you know ours will fail?" she asked.

"Mine always do. I'm a mess."

"Then let's not have a relationship. Let's just fuck."

"Wow. Such language and no maiden's blush to bepaint thy cheek."

She blinked. Twice. "What?"

"I'm misquoting Shakespeare. You saw me at the baseball game. With another woman."

"I did."

"It bothered you."

"So?" she said.

"If you and I are only physical, it wouldn't have."

"I got a little jealous. Get over it. Who is she, anyway?"

"A girl I'm smitten with."

She released my hand. "Smitten? What the hell."

"I know. I'm practically a Jane Austen character. But I'm not dating her so I don't know what to call it."

"Is she smitten with you?"

"She is."

She didn't appreciably move but her entire being seemed to bend away from me. "Then why did you invite me over?"

"I enjoy your company. And I told you I would."

"So this is, like, charity?"

"Not at all."

"I'm a grown woman, Mack. Not some chaste fifteen-year-old girl, coming over to chat with a boy. I have needs."

"Me too. But sex no longer satisfies that need."

"You want to get married." She snorted. "Live happily ever after."

"Maybe even put up a picket fence."

"God."

"I'm so unenlightened it's breathtaking," I said. "I'm not smart enough to know if casual sex is possible. I make no judgements. This is not a prescription on how life should be lived; it's a description of who I am."

She took a deep breath and let it out. As though reluctantly coming to terms with the Neanderthal she'd chosen. "So anytime I want sex from you I'm required to ambush you. Take off my clothes so you're unable to resist. Slide the cocaine under your nose, so to speak."

"That'd do the trick but I do not advocate that approach. If you're simply after a physical sensation you could find any number of willing private detectives."

"I don't want them," she said.

"Why not."

"I want you."

"I cannot blame you. My heart is pure and I know not fear."

"That another poem?"

"Yes, though, again, I've butchered it."

"And I've butchered casual sex, admitting I want it from you and not from others. I suppose it's easier said than done." She was leaning toward me again. The defensive wall had dissipated.

"Much of life is."

"So you want to date both me and what's-her-name?"

"I'm not dating her. Nor will I, anytime soon."

"Why not?" she asked.

"She's getting married. To someone other than me."

"Oh Mack." She grinned. As though taking pleasure in my character faults. "You filthy tomcat."

"She and I have not, ahh, been intimate."

"Really? You fucked me and not her?"

"Not exactly Hallmark phrasing but yes."

"Okay. I can live with that." She nodded to herself. "You know, not every college instructor would be willing to bang a guy with a kid. You're lucky."

"Because a kid is baggage."

"Obviously."

"Not to me. To me he's pure light."

"Whatever. You're going to keep avoiding my sexual advances?" she asked.

"To the best of my abilities."

"Are you with me only to get your mind off her?"

"I don't know. I can't rule out that possibility."

She shrugged and picked up her beer.

"Beggars can't be choosers, I guess," she said.

"Kristin. You're not a beggar. Have a look in the mirror. Walk into a bar and take your pick of suitors."

"Gross. What kind of girl do you take me for?"

"The sexually voracious kind."

"You got that right, Mack."

19

I walked onto the Patrick Henry football field and shook hands with Ricky Alexander, head coach of the Patriots. He was tall and thick, like he played offensive lineman in college and kept the bulk. Meaty hands. Goatee. Friendly voice, strong but held in check.

"Mack, you going to coach my defense or what?"

"Long as you understand. I have a weird job with weird hours," I said.

He wore a purple and gold windbreaker and a purple hat. School colors. "We can work around that. So you're in?"

"I'm in. Try it for a season and see how we fit."

"Excellent. You and I can meet sometime soon. Talk philosophies of winning. What I'm looking for most of all is a defensive-minded role model. We'll have forty kids trying out for defense. Thirty of them will have unmarried parents. Twenty of them will have no contact with their father or have fathers in jail. Ten of them will have never met their father. You get it?"

"We're doing more than teaching football. That's the only reason I agreed," I said.

"Then you and I are on the same page."

"Could be the beginning of a beautiful friendship."

He grinned and smacked a clipboard against my chest. "Don't get weird on me. Let's just coach the hell out of this team."

He moved away and I stood on the sidelines, examining the roster for names I already knew. A black Lexus LS pulled into the parking lot. Marcus Morgan emerged from the driver's side and Fat Susie lumbered out the passenger. Marcus was dressed in black slacks and a black turtleneck and he walked to me with deliberate and measured steps.

"Your wardrobe," I said. "Must make for a boring closet."

"The fewer choices I make in the morning the better."

"Ah. Limited brainpower."

"Something like that," he said. "You the new coach?"

"Defensive coordinator."

"Excellent. Thank you."

"Not doing it for you."

He had silver sunglasses on. The school reflected off the mirrored surface. "I know. Thank you, just the same."

"You come to all the practices?"

"Many as I can. Not enough."

"Got time for a professional question?" I asked.

"I do."

"What will Calvin do with the informant, once I find him?"

"You sure you'll find him?"

"Seventy-five percent chance," I said.

"Summers'll do what he should do. He'll do what I would do. Or come close."

"What would you do?"

"Handcuff him. Take an ax to him. Take a chainsaw to him. Make people watch," he said. Like he was discussing a hamburger recipe.

"Marcus. Perhaps you need to watch less violent television."

He grinned and fiddled with the silver watch on his left wrist. "It's not pleasant. But someone sent me to prison?" Shook his head and grunted. "I burn their house down, too."

"You've done the ax thing before?"

"Only once. I was twenty-six. Haven't been betrayed since."

"Still. Seems excessive."

"You don't got the heart for it, do you," he said. "You're balking. Don't want the responsibility on your shoulders. Blood on your hands. I told Calvin maybe you weren't the right guy for the job."

"But a chainsaw? No way. That only happens in *Scarface*."

"You want in the underworld? This comes with the territory."

"Who said I wanted in the underworld?" I asked.

"Too late now, August. You're in. And you're in thick."

"I should have been consulted first. I decline the invitation."

"On the bright side, we pay good."

"You pay in chainsaws," I said.

"Only those who betray us. You got nothing to worry about."

Was I one degree less masculine, my hands holding the clipboard would have trembled. Because I planned on betraying Calvin. "Does Fat Susie know about the axes and chainsaws?"

"Course. Who you think will hold the handle?"

"Poor Fat Susie," I said. "He'll have PTSD."

"Don't feel bad for Fat Susie. Feel bad for the informant. Mother-fucker's gonna have a rough spring."

20

Motherfucker's gonna have a rough Spring.

He's going to be tied up and killed with axes and chainsaws while others watch. Because he betrayed the Mafioso.

And I was supposed to deliver said betrayer to the ax-wielding lunatics. If I quit or if I found out who it was and I kept my mouth shut then I became a betrayer too.

And I hated being killed with chainsaws.

These were the pleasant thoughts keeping me company as I did a job for Moseley Law Firm. He needed statements taken by a third party and that's exactly what I did. I took them so good, well into the evening. Timothy August picked Kix up from Roxanne's and I worked late.

I swung by my office on the way home around nine that night. On warm nights like this, downtown Roanoke felt more like a step backwards in time than a modern city. A safer and simpler time, when couples held hands under the streetlights and live music spilled out of restaurants. Which was exactly what I saw on the corner of Campbell and Market — a live band inside the hookah bar and couples leaning into each other.

Star City of the South indeed.

I creaked and squeaked up the stairs. Unlocked the door. Flipped the light switch. Went in.

A man stood to my right. I detected him in my periphery. The intruder's back was flat against the wall and he was hoping I'd pass him by unnoticed.

I elbowed him. Violent and sudden, driving my hard ulna bone into his solar plexus. He made a noise like a confused gasp and he doubled over.

His face looked familiar.

His eyes flickered to someone behind me.

I spun away. A heavy something caught me on the left shoulder, instead of catching me in the skull.

It hurt. But I remained conscious. Like Achilles would have.

Another man was there. A man even more pathetic in appearance. Unfamiliar and looking unsure what to do.

I put a fist into his throat and heard the wretched crunch of cartilage. He gagged.

Scott. That was the first guy's name, the superintendent of Happy Hills trailer park. Scott came up holding his chest, which hurt like everything. In his other hand he held a heavy revolver. I took the revolver in my fist and bent his wrist inward until the barrel was aimed at his own chest.

Neither man wanted to kill me. Not really. Perhaps they'd been sent here to do that but they didn't *want* to. They weren't trained or hardened to the task. If so it could have been done easily when I walked in. Killing a man requires a lot of work, most of it emotional.

The unknown intruder kept gagging. He scrambled out of my reach. He had a gun too. A Glock.

I kept steady pressure on Scott's revolver. He squirmed helplessly. With my other hand, my left, I withdrew my pistol and aimed it at the gagging unknown intruder.

He aimed at me.

I aimed at him.

Scott aimed at Scott.

"Call it a truce?" I asked. Politely.

"Jesus," the intruder said. His throat was damaged and he sounded like a dog straining and coughing against a leash. He twisted, feeling vulnerable and scared under my gun. "Don't shoot, man!"

Was I scared?

Not I. I felt no fear.

Mostly because I thought his safety was still engaged.

"Put your gun on my desk and I won't," I said.

He fired. A shocking blast in my enclosed office.

The bullet punched a small hole through the drywall to the left of my head. He'd missed.

So I was wrong about the safety.

My ears rang and Scott shouted something.

I aimed — with a steady left hand — and returned fire. Another ear-splitting pop.

The bullet grazed the acromion bone, adjacent to his clavicle. Pulp misted from his shoulder. The shot only nicked him, drilling another bullet hole in my office, but the impact spun him 180 degrees and his legs gave out. His pistol landed in the corner.

"I'm hit!" he cried.

"You shot him!"

"Scott," I said. "Release your revolver and tend to your friend."

"You shot him," Scott told me again.

"Indeed. Now he needs steady pressure on that shoulder. Let go. And help him."

"What?" said Scott. Poor thing, he was overcome by my aim and strength and general masculinity.

"Let go," I said.

He did.

"Now take your shirt off."

"Why?"

"A bandage."

He complied.

"Now press it firmly onto the wound."

"You ain't gonna kill us?"

"Not today, Scott. Who's your friend?"

Scott crouched next to the man and pressed the shirt into his wound. The man did not react to the pressure with grace and courage.

Scott said, "Aw shut up, Parks. It's a scratch."

"Fuck you, a scratch. I been shot."

I collected Parks's Glock from the corner. Put both it and the revolver onto my shelf.

I asked, "How many nights have you been waiting here?"

"Only three."

"Wayne sent you?"

"Ain't gotta tell you nothing."

I eased the hammer down on my 1911. Ejected the clip. Examined it. Jacked it in again. Thumbed the hammer back with a heavy click. The cacophony of sound was mellifluous. And effective. They watched with white faces.

"You two are going home. And telling Wayne what?" I asked. "That I beat you up? Took your guns? What are you going to report?"

No response.

"I bet you a dollar it won't be the truth," I said.

The man with the wounded shoulder winced and sat up straighter.

"So I'll call Wayne now and tell him what happened. And I'll keep your guns," I said. "Or. You tell me who sent you and why, and you can tell Wayne whatever falsehood you like and I'll only keep your ammunition."

"Wayne sent us," Parks said.

Scott cursed. The really bad word.

"Why," I said.

"To kill you," he said. "Or 'least shoot you."

"Why."

"Dunno. Don't tell us nothing."

"I think it's because he's hiding something. What do you think?"

"Maybe cause you're a sonovabitch."

"You guys take orders from Calvin Summers?" I asked.

"Sure," Scott said.

"Who?" Parks asked. "Dunno Summers."

Scott worked at Happy Hills so it made sense he'd know Calvin. Parks appeared authentically confused by the name, which interested me.

"Parks, you know Deputy Yopp?" I asked. "Fat mean bastard?"

"Yeah, I know Yopp."

"Does Deputy Yopp work with Calvin Summers?"

"Dunno no Summers," Parks said again. "Doubt it."

"Yeah me too." I scratched at my jaw with the sight of my pistol. "Wayne does a lot of business without consulting Calvin Summers, I'm beginning to realize. Is that right, Scott?"

Scott shrugged. "Dunno. I just work Happy Hills."

"You just work Happy Hills."

"Right."

"You guys think Wayne could beat me up?" I asked.

No response.

"Keep in mind, I'm not even flexing," I said.

"Wayne kick your ass."

"Agree to disagree. Does Wayne ever bring cocaine to your trailer park?"

"Cocaine? Naw, ain't got no cocaine."

"Just moonshine and weed and prescription pills," I said.

"Yep."

"I think Wayne is hiding something. But I don't know what," I said. "There's something he's not telling me. Something he's hiding from Calvin Summers. Why else would he want me dead?"

The two good ol' boys remained quiet.

"Aside from his overwhelming jealousy, I mean. Of all things Mackenzie."

I emptied the revolver's cylinder. Scott had only loaded four bullets, which hurt my feelings. Surely I looked like I required more than four. I emptied the Glock's chamber and magazine and handed them their weapons.

"Go back. Tell Wayne you hit me in the head until I no longer moved. Tell him I bled and whimpered. And you two don't come back. Whaddaya say?"

Instead of answering, they avoided my eye contact and made for the door. Gregarious couple. They limped out, holding various parts of their bodies.

I said, "When you recall this night to your children, and I know that you will, I'd like to be shirtless and have tattoos up and down my arms. Okay? Guys? Okay?"

I watched their old truck rattle to life and cough its way toward 581. Remove the rust, they'd be left with a steering wheel and four tires. On a sudden whim, I dashed to my car.

"Dash" might be too strong a word. I moved to my car as quickly as old football knees would allow and wondered again if I should join a CrossFit box.

I knew where Scott lived. I didn't know much else at the moment, but the man had tried to kill me so this appeared to be a potential lead. I passed their truck five miles out of town and plunged into the dark country roads of Franklin County.

I arrived at Happy Fields first. The four overhead lamps which should have bathed the entire park in an ambient glow were all broken. I parked inside a thicket of pine, turned off the lights, and crept closer to Scott's trailer.

Should have brought pit bull repellant.

A woman was inside Scott's trailer. She watched an Adam Sandler movie on Netflix with her bare feet propped on the coffee table. She looked jittery and exhausted and angry. I watched her through the torn screen of the storm door and I solved the case doing so.

I wished. In fact, I learned absolutely nothing except that she was most likely addicted to cigarettes. Her fingers kept going to her lips on habit.

Scott came home ten minutes later without Parks. His truck door

squealed and squawked and he stumped inside without a glance at
me hidden in the shadows.

"The hell you been," the girl said.

"Out."

"Yeah I know, out. Where?"

"Out. Doing stuff for Wayne."

"Doing stuff for Wayne," she mocked him. "Little boy, grow some
balls. Stop being a bitch for Wayne."

"He's my friend. And my boss. You want me to lose my job?"

"What'd he want you for?"

Scott didn't reply. He went into the kitchen, which was separated
from the television room by a counter, and he put a cigarette into his
mouth.

"You hear me?" she said. "Stop being a little bitch. God, you're
stupid. Hey gimme one them cigarettes."

Scott tossed her one. She fumbled the catch but picked it off the
floor and lit it. She said, "We're outta shine."

"Get some more tomorrow."

"Get some more tomorrow," she repeated in a high voice. "With
what money?"

"I got a little bit."

"Just go get some from the storage unit."

"That ain't ours," Scott said.

"Fuck you, that ain't ours. You're the boss, dickhead. Go get some."

"I ain't."

"Gimme the keys then."

"No. That ain't ours. Wayne would know."

She rolled her eyes and bounced on the couch with an irritated
huff. "Wayne Wayne Wayne. Maybe I should be Wayne's girlfriend."

"Good fucking luck. He's got a girl twice as good as you."

"I hate this place. I hate this shitty place," she said.

"Can't you shut up? I had a bad night."

"Oh you had a bad night? Poor little bitch. We're outta shine.
Maybe you had a real job."

"No one's ever asked you to stay," Scott mumbled.

"Maybe I'll leave."

"Uh-huh. Why do you watch this stupid shit?"

"Maybe I'll leave, Scott."

"Get on. You'll be back in the morning. Lauren gets a' sick of you as I do," he said. He was staring at the floor, leaning forward with his hands on the counter, head between his elbows.

"Ain't going to Lauren's. I'll go be the nigger's girlfriend."

Scott chuckled and emitted puffs of blue smoke around his ears. "Craig? Craig's wrinkled ass is seventy."

"He be glad to have me. Bet Craig's got shine."

"Get on then."

The girl stood up and announced, "You're a dickless sonovabitch, you know that. And you can go to hell."

Scott didn't reply.

The screen door closed weakly after her. She stormed off into the dark, stomping on cold grass with thin legs.

Scott set the revolver onto the counter and moved in front of the television. He pinched the bridge of his nose between his eyes and took the cigarette out of his mouth.

I flung open the screen door and stepped into the room. It's important to make a good entrance.

Scott said, "Holy shit."

"Ta daaaa."

"You followed me."

"A magician never reveals his secrets," I said.

"Man I'm about sick of you."

"I get that a lot. Fortunately I don't believe it. Wow this place reeks of ash. I think I just got lung cancer."

"What do you want," Scott said.

"You know why Summers hired me?"

"Yeah. Find the snitch."

"Correct. And I've decided it's not you."

"No shit. I'm tired, man. Let me get to sleep," he said.

"Scott. Educate me. I don't get this part of Franklin County."

"What's that mean?"

"It means...I don't know what it means. Help me understand. Why do you live like this?" I sat down on the wooden armrest of the heavy chair. The cushion looked like it'd swallow me.

"Like what?"

"You could work on a dairy farm and wait tables at night. Start making better money and get a nicer truck. Find a girl who won't scream at you. Take classes at the community college. Move into an apartment."

"The hell I want an apartment for?" he asked. "I was born here."

"You grew up in Happy Fields?"

"Hey dumbass, I was born *here*. In this trailer."

"You're kidding."

"No I ain't," he said. He lit a new cigarette off the final red ashes of his first. "When I say I was born here, I mean I was born here."

"As in, you were delivered inside this trailer?"

"Still got a stain on the bedroom carpet. Probably die in the same room. Ain't never been to a doctor."

"Not once?"

"Not once, not even for a broken arm. Couldn't afford it. Set it myself and wrapped it with boards. School nurse never said a thing."

"Where's your mom?" I asked and I had the curious feeling of becoming a more pronounced horse's ass with each word.

"Jail. Rehab. Somewhere, I don't know. Ain't seen her in years. Been on my own since I was fifteen."

"The social workers allowed that?" I asked.

"They don't know nothing."

"What about your father?"

"Never met the fucker," Scott said. "Ran off. And I can't take classes. Never graduated. Bus quit coming by and I had to work. Wasn't passing anything, no ways. I'm a hard worker. Always been. But not so good at school."

"Ah," I said. Yep. I was a horse's ass.

"And that girl? She ain't my girlfriend. Used to be a hooker. She's stayed here about a month and storms off once a week. She'll be gone 'fore you know it. I hope. Sick of supporting her."

We were silent while Adam Sandler made stupid jokes on screen with the same group of buddies he always did. Scott quit watching. The cigarette smoldered in his fist and he stared at the ceiling.

"Scott, considering everything you've just told me, I owe you an apology."

"Yeah?"

"Life dealt you a bad starting hand. About a rough as it gets. And yet you've got a job, a place to live, and a working car. You're loyal to your boss and it looks like you don't hit your girl and you don't steal. I was looking at you all wrong and I'm sorry."

"Man's got to have some rules for hisself."

"I'll try to remember that. And I won't pester you any longer."

"Lock the door on your way out," he said. "I'm tired of that girl's mouth running."

"I don't blame you."

21

Early the following morning I rented a truck from the local Enterprise. I asked for an '84 Chevy pickup with rust stains. The lady at the desk did not smile; she informed me that she had a brand-new Nissan Frontier. Would that do?

I supposed it would. Not perfect camouflage but better than my toy car. To complete the disguise I wore a baseball cap. Foolproof.

I wanted to examine Wayne's house. To break and enter while he was without. But that required observing it until he left, which necessitated the risk of being discovered, and he knew what my car looked like. So I planned on sitting in my rented truck until he passed. This truck was like a hunting blind for guys like Wayne. His eyes would pass right over me. He'd see the truck and my ball cap and think, "Yup, that looks about right."

An hour later, as I neared Wayne's bend in the road, the man himself came roaring around the turn. His monster truck occupied most of the road and he was shouting into his phone. He charged by without giving my truck a second glance and disappeared over the hill.

"Eureka," I said.

I moved briskly. I pulled into his driveway and hopped out. The house was small and brick, maybe an eight hundred square foot main level. The yard was scrub and gravel and vines. Hoses and metal parts and an old grill rotted in his backyard.

The side door was unlocked. It opened into a kitchen with a linoleum floor. Trash bags in the corners overflowed with beer cans, Styrofoam coffee cups, and Bojangles bags. An old table with one chair was loaded with boxes of Miller Lite. The barren pantry contained hot chocolate and a jar of cheap marinara sauce.

In the adjacent room, a woman slept on a ratty brown couch. She was dressed in a T-shirt and G-string. She was so thin and pallid I could see blue veins in her cheeks and forehead. Her mouth hung open and she snored. Her hair had been bleached to the point of straw. On the coffee table was an entire apothecary of pill bottles.

Her phone buzzed.

I moved deeper into the house. Wayne's bedroom was thoroughly uninteresting. A twin bed. Stained sheets on the floor. A television. That was it. The bathroom produced such a stench that I examined it from the hall, shirt collar pulled over my nose.

I found the basement stairs and descended. I yanked on a cord and the overhead light buzzed on. The walls were painted cinder block. His hot water heater clanked noisily.

Two safes sat on either side of an old metal desk. On the left was a gun safe, the kind with a glass window. It wasn't locked. Wayne had an impressive arsenal of illegal assault rifles. He appeared ready to fight off a zombie invasion. Or Hillary Clinton, should she rise again. There was a small built-in box at the bottom and a set of keys rested inside.

The second safe was smaller and it was locked. On a whim, I took the keys from the gun safe and inserted them into the locked safe. Click. The door swung open.

Stacks of money spilled out. Tens and twenties bound by rubber bands. Fifty thousand dollars? A hundred? Maybe more.

This proved nothing. Calvin might know about it. But still, the plot thickened. I didn't know if Wayne was the informant but he was clearly a person of interest.

With all this money he should be paying Scott more. The kid had grown on me.

I rifled through papers on his desk. Water and electric bills from Happy Fields and Glade Hill Acres and Ferrum's Fields. Printed emails. Handwritten notes. Receipts.

I found a list of nine names and corresponding phone numbers. All of the names were girls.

Rose Long
Robyn Elliot
Alicia Gordon
Michelle Doyle
Pamela Stevens
Etc.

I took a photograph of the names. And of the bills. And of a few other notes.

On my way out, I passed the sleeping girl. Her phone buzzed again with incoming text messages. I glanced at the message because I was a professional investigator. Not because I was creepy.

The message was from Michelle.

Could it be Michelle Doyle, from the list in the basement? Michelle was asking (with significant urgency and vulgarity) where she was supposed to go. I scrolled through recent messages. Michelle often asked the question, "Where do I go?" and she was given various destinations I didn't recognize.

Hmmm, I thought. What would FBI Jamie do at this point? Probably something fancy with the phone.

I searched through the phone's contacts. I found a Rose and a Robyn and an Alicia and all the rest. Alicia had texted yesterday and she'd been told to go to Ferrum's Fields tomorrow morning. Ferrum's Fields, the upscale trailer park.

The girl asleep on the couch (I deduced her name was either Vickie or Bitch) was weekly giving these girls instructions on where to go.

Go here. Go there. Get back to me. Where are you?
And I thought, "Huh."
Another befuddling clue.
Or a ploy to throw me off track. That Wayne was a sly one.
And I easy to befuddle.

22

I kept the truck for an additional day and I parked it outside Ferrum's Fields, near the entrance so I could observe the shenanigans. My cap was on. My tires had gotten a little muddy. I tuned to a country radio station to further imbed myself in character.

Mackenzie August. Southern gentleman.

After an hour of watching the lazy comings and goings of the residents I spotted who I thought was Alicia Gordon. A thin girl, maybe twenty, who spent fifteen minutes in a trailer, came outside, smoked a cigarette, trudged to a different trailer and repeated the process.

She was a prostitute. Providing her services to approximately ten of the fifty trailers within the park. She wore old jeans and a white tank top. A heavy handbag was slung around her shoulders and her hair was up.

She finished at one, an hour after my normal lunch and I was hungry. She marched up the gentle slope leading out of the trailer park and turned east toward Rocky Mount. I eased the truck next to her, window down, and said, "Hi Alicia Gordon."

She was busily typing on her phone with both thumbs and she barely spared me a frown. "What? Who the *hell* you."

"Yikes. You fit a discouraging amount of disdain into that word," I said.

"Huh?"

"I work with Calvin Summers. Can I give you a lift?"

"No. Who's Calvin Summers?" she said, still walking, still looking at her phone. "Dumbass rich name."

"He owns the trailer park. Never heard of him? Works with Wayne Cross? You know Wayne?"

"Course I know Wayne."

"And you know Vickie," I said.

"Duh."

Alicia was too thin and drawn. Her face had the pinched look of a hard upbringing. Her clothes were old and her hair needed professional intervention and her makeup was too heavy and I saw tattoos on her ankles. She was nasty and mean, but life had given her little reason to be otherwise. Or so I surmised.

"Get in," I said. "I'll buy you lunch."

She stopped and sighed. "Why."

"For the pleasure of your company."

"Fuck you mister, I ain't blowing you in your truck. I'm tired."

"Ah. No. You misunderstand. My mistake. What I meant to say was let's get lunch, my treat, nothing required of you. As I told you, I work for the owner of the Ferrum's Fields. Afterwards I'll drop you off anywhere you want."

Her arms crossed. "You a cop?"

"I'm not. Promise. Where you headed?"

"My girlfriend's house, down the way. I stay there till she gets off work and she takes me home."

"Come on. Let's get lunch," I said. "You answer a few questions about the trailer park and we'll call it even."

"Fine, whatever." She stomped around to the passenger seat and climbed in. "This a pretty boy truck. Not good for much."

"Where to?"

"Duh. Dairy Queen."

"Silly me," I said.

The restaurant was off Highway 40, near Ferrum College. She ordered a chicken tender meal with fries and a Mountain Dew. I got a chili dog.

She ate without looking at me. She chewed and skimmed down her Facebook timeline.

"You used to work here, didn't you," I said.

"How'd you know?"

"This place and the supermarket are the only two places around."

"I worked there too."

"You like what you do now, instead of working at the supermarket?" I asked.

"Pays better. I guess."

I asked, "How'd you meet Vickie?"

"Through Wayne."

"How'd you meet Wayne?"

"Everybody know Wayne," she said. "Wayne's Wayne."

"He treat you well?"

"I guess."

"Does he pay you enough?"

"Hell naw he doesn't," she said. "For what I do? Shit. Not enough money."

"Are you from Franklin County?"

"Course I am. Why you asking these stupid questions?"

"I'm friendly," I said.

"Yeah. Well. Just keep your dick zipped up, okay mister. What'cha bring me here for, anyway?" Still she didn't look at me. She started playing with the gold hoop in her right earlobe.

I detected that Alicia did not love Wayne. That she had to tell all of Wayne's friends to keep their pants zipped up. That maybe I could be a little more honest with her and not get burned.

Or it could be the chili dog giving me hope.

"I work for Wayne's boss," I said.

"So."

"And I wonder sometimes if Wayne steals from him."

"Oh. Sure he does. Wayne'd steal his granny's government checks, she let him. Wayne steals from everybody." She pronounced it, "ehhbody."

"Has he ever talked about his boss?"

"Don't know. Wayne's mean, mister. Be careful, I was you."

"He's a big guy," I said.

"Yep."

"I'm big too."

Perhaps for the first time she looked at me. She glanced at my shoulders. My arms. My neck. My face. "Yeah. Yeah you're big. Why you so big?"

"I did a couple pushups last month."

"Huh?"

"If he's such a jerk, why do you work for him?" I asked.

"Gotta eat. What else should I do." She was back to her phone and her golden earring.

"What—"

"I'm the dumb one, mister. My family's got important jobs. My sister's a secretary. My mom drives a school bus. Me? I service old guys who smell like cheese. You think I like what I do? 'Cause I don't."

"Do you live with your family?"

"Live with my boyfriend," she said.

"Does he work for Wayne?"

"No, he's a drunk bum. Hurt his foot riding four-wheelers. Can't even get disability. Been thinking 'bout leaving him. Hits me, he gets mad."

"Have you ever seen Wayne talking with an older guy? Good looking, silver hair, dresses like a fancy rich guy?" I asked.

"Nope, no fancy rich guys. I wish. Might pay better."

"Your customers pay you directly?"

"Naw. Wayne pays me."

"Do you know any of the other girls who work with Wayne?" I asked.

"Sure, some."

"Any of them hate Wayne? Might talk with me?"

"No. We don't hate Wayne. He's okay. Better'n most, I guess."

"Do you know Scott?" I asked.

"Scott at Happy Hills."

"Yes."

"I know Scott. Nice guy, but he's got a girlfriend. Why?"

"Here's what I think," I said, but I was interrupted. By a woman. She was short. Probably sixty but her hair was still completely brown. A small plain face, but determined. No makeup. She wore a dress, the kind with a faux apron sewn on, and sandals with socks.

"Alicia," she said. "Alicia I'm taking you home." She spoke in short fierce syllabic bursts, loud enough that the patrons stared.

Alicia nodded her head, like a schoolgirl getting caught by the principal. All the mean prostitute bravado had vanished. She looked at me again. "Sorry mister. Gotta go. Thanks for lunch."

"You're welcome."

The fiery older woman said, "Now Alicia."

"Yes Mrs. Hunt," Alicia said.

Mrs. Hunt. I knew that name.

"Collect your things. Throw away your trash. Wait in the car," she said.

"Yes Mrs. Hunt."

The woman waited, eyes fixed on me until Alicia had walked outside and gotten into her old Subaru.

"You. Outside."

"Yes Mrs. Hunt," I said.

I threw away my trash under her watchful eye and followed her into the parking lot feeling strangely penitent.

"I know who you are," she said.

"And I know you. You're Boyd's wife and you operate the dairy farm," I said proudly. Maybe I'd get a gold star.

"You've got no right. No right to bother these girls."

"But—"

"I know who you are," she said again. "You're working for that Calvin Summers. You fooled Mr. Hunt, with your talk of expansion. But not me. You're up to something and it's not good. And you've got no right."

"Perhaps there is more to this story than—"

"Oh, I've done my homework. You live in the city. Come down here. Think you know better. Think you're superior. Think all your education and modernization is salvation, gives you the right to exploit us," she said. Her hands were gripped together and every few words they'd flex and tug. "You look down on girls like Alicia. Think she's helpless and pathetic. I don't know what your goal is but I hate it. You're too busy to notice you'll get people hurt."

"I'm not going to get Alicia hurt," I said.

"Stop working for Calvin Summers. Stop this instant, you've no right."

"I can't stop. But—"

"You're going to hurt someone innocent."

"Maybe not," I said.

Passersby watched us from their cars and from the sidewalk. We made quite the show. I wished she'd keep her voice down. I didn't embarrass easily but she'd done the trick.

"Let Alicia alone. Let the other girls alone."

"How do you know them?"

"I live here." She practically bit the words off and threw them at me. "You don't. They weren't born with silver spoons. They're doing the best they can with what they were given and the last thing they need is you snooping around."

"You know what Alicia does for a living," I said. It was half a question, half a statement.

"Of course. Everyone knows."

"You approve?"

"Don't be a fool. Of course not. You're no better than Calvin Summers, trying to make money off us. It's not Alicia's fault. Calvin wants to exploit her and so do you and so do the awful men in those awful places and I wish you'd all just let her alone."

We glared at each other for a minute.

Well. She glared. I tried not to wither.

I said, "I'm not here to make trouble for Alicia."

"You're a hired thug. And you're bringing trouble with you."

"What further trouble could she possible get into? I'm trying to help."

"She don't need help from the city. She needs her family. She needs to bottom out and take some responsibility. There aren't quick solutions in real life."

"How do you help?" I asked.

"I help her fill out job applications. I clean her up when she gets beat. By men like you."

"Men like me put our kids to bed at seven thirty and watch a ball game until nine when we're exhausted. Men like me are starting to grow hair on our ears and we don't know why. We don't hit girls."

She sniffed.

"You're her family?" I asked.

"Not by blood. May as well be. Leastwise I live here. Unlike you."

A chasm of inexpressible misunderstandings separated us. I couldn't explain to her my ulterior motives for working for Calvin Summers. Not here in a parking lot. And even if I tried she wouldn't believe me. I could think of nothing to say. So I went with that.

"Calvin Summers is a bad man," she said.

"Yes ma'am."

"You work for him? So are you."

"Yes ma'am."

She scowled. "You want to help? Go back to Roanoke. And stay there."

"For what it's worth, I don't think Calvin Summers is Alicia's employer. I think Wayne Cross is running that show without Calvin's permission."

"Don't mean Calvin Summers is a good man. He should still be rotting in jail. And so should that Wayne Cross. I'll ring the sheriff again, not like it does a lot of good."

"You've called the sheriff on Calvin?"

"Of course I have. I've done everything I can think of to help these girls."

She stomped to her Subaru and slammed the door.

As the car drove off I heard Mrs. Hunt haranguing Alicia on the folly of her ways.

I'd finally found someone who hated Calvin Summers, and she'd even called the cops on him.

She was kinda great. Even if she hated me.

23

Kix and I went for a jog. From our house it was only a mile to the greenway, paradise for plodding runners such as myself. The daffodils had begun to fade and tulips threatened to bloom. The tulips wouldn't last long because Roanoke had a bizarre urban deer population which lived almost exclusively on tulips. I could purchase a bow and arrow and kill a deer a day and eat deer sausage for every meal and it wouldn't make a dent.

I ran a mile and a half each way on the greenway and finished at the playground with the big green alligator near Black Dog Salvage. I sat on a bench in the shade of a budding oak tree and panted and sweated profusely.

Kix stared at me with bottomless eyes.

We need to talk, he said.

"About what?"

You know.

"About Kristin."

Obviously.

"You don't like Kristin."

And you don't like her much either.

"She's fun," I said.

He looked away from me and took a long drink from his juice bottle. I'd started to mix his juice with water because he'd gotten a little heavy in the cheeks. He slammed it back onto the tray. *She's fun.*

"Well..."

She's FUN??

"Not a great reason, I know. But she's pretty. She's successful. Well educated."

So is Condoleezza Rice. Date her.

"Condoleezza doesn't like me. Kristin does."

You're lowering your standards.

I wiped my forehead with my shirt. The breeze had an edge and the sweat would make me shiver soon. "You're right. I've lowered my standards. But that doesn't mean Kristin can't be great."

You say that because you're lonely.

"I know this."

That's crap. We got a good thing going, the August boys.

"Not a good thing, a great thing."

What about Ronnie?

"What about her? She's getting married to another man."

...and?

"Kix. Don't be a scoundrel."

The girl is into you.

"So."

More importantly, she's into me.

"She's got great taste."

She does. Way better than what's-her-name. Remember when what's-her-name asked how to shut me up?

"You mean Kristin."

Yes. That one.

"Ronnie's a mess, Kix. She's in at least two relationships which aren't healthy. She doesn't need a third. Because then I'd get mixed up in the mess too."

You already are.

"I know. Let me finish this case for her father. Then I'll think about the other stuff."

Wimp.

"I believe the word you're searching for is cautious."

Wimp.

"Somebody wants an earlier bedtime tonight."

Tell Ronnie you love her.

"Love her?"

The heart wants what it wants.

"You're about to lose Elmo privileges."

Fine. Let's talk about something else. Speaking of getting mixed up into messes, how about you working for crime bosses?

"Just one crime boss. And he's the least of them."

Don't try to explain it away. That's a tactic for lesser men.

"When I took the case I didn't know Calvin was connected with the underworld."

This is a bold career choice. Becoming a hit man.

"I'm not a hit man."

Kinda.

"I didn't choose it. Soon as I finish this, I'm done with them."

I doubt it.

"I doubt it too. Marcus Morgan seems to think I'm already thick with the thieves."

Manny thinks so too.

"Manny is a maniac. He'd like for us to get into gun battles most weekends."

Considering you are my primary care provider, I cannot approve of gun battles. Wait. Do I get all your stuff if you die?

"Not till you're eighteen."

I cannot approve of gun battles.

We paused our existential conversation while two women power-walked nearby. They smiled at us. We smiled back. Kix examined their muscular structure after they'd passed. I shook my finger at him. He shrugged.

You keep talking about finishing the case.

"Yeah?"

You think Mrs. Hunt is the informant.

"It makes sense. She hates Summers. She's called the police on him. She thinks he should still be in jail. She's connected to the money. Summers bought her farm and she didn't approve. It's gotta be her."

So you'll turn her over to Calvin Summers and his chainsaws?

"What a morbid little mind you have."

Maybe you shouldn't watch Law & Order while I'm in the room.

"I'm not turning her in to Calvin."

Then you're breaking your promise to him. And that goes against who you are.

"Who I am?"

You value responsibility. Truth. Honesty.

"What about my responsibility to the innocent? Innocent people like Mrs. Hunt?"

You're the detective, not me. I am simply an observer. And I observe your conscience won't let you betray your client to such an extent.

"You're right. I can't completely betray my client."

Yes.

"But I also won't hand Mrs. Hunt over to be slaughtered."

Quite a pickle you're in, old man.

"If it's even her."

It's her.

"You're just guessing."

He yawned.

"Maybe you should take a nap," I said.

He grinned. The little boy grin I adored.

Heck of an idea. Get my stroller moving. I like a little motion.

I stood, stretched, and started pushing toward home. "Thanks Kix. You've given me some clarity."

What are you going to do? About the informant.

"I'm not sure. I'm not positive it's Mrs. Hunt."

But.

Now that I thought about it...

I knew a remedy for that.

24

Bill Osborne the federal prosecutor arrived at Billy's at precisely 5:30pm. I stood at the bar drinking a gin and ginger and watching a Cubs game wind down. Bill didn't dress like some other US attorneys I'd met. Federal guys were alpha dogs, power players, dressed to kill and grind down any injustice which needed grinding. The bar was dark and he didn't notice me at first. The bartender brought him a scotch without being asked. Bill sat on the stool, twitched his shoulders, and sipped his drink and loosened his tie. He took a deep breath and glanced at the television before returning to his phone screen.

The bartender was just a kid, maybe twenty-five. Jeez, when did twenty-five-year-olds become kids? This guy kept his hair long and pulled back. He wanted to grow a beard but it wasn't happening. I finished my gin and set the glass down heavily.

"Another?" the kid asked.

"Please," I said.

Distracted by our witty banter, Bill Osborne glanced up and recognized me.

"Hey," he said. "You're the guy. The private detective."

"Of all the gin joints in all the world..."

"Mack. That's it. August. Mack August, how's it going."

I shook his hand. Too limp. Did no one tell this guy how kick-ass federal attorneys were supposed to be?

The bartender gave me another and wandered off.

"Bill," I said. "I hope you had a full day of defending the American way."

"Not exactly. I'm a prosecutor."

"Then your soul to the devil, sir."

He grinned and drank more scotch. "Still working with Calvin Summers?"

"I am. What a pain in the ass that guy is."

"Damn right. I mostly worked with Ronnie but one time I met with him? Guy asked me to get him a coffee."

"What'd you say?"

"Fuck you, is what I said." He twitched his shoulders and picked up his phone. "I told you to be careful with him, right?"

"You did. And it was good advice. Calvin's better connected than I assumed."

"I told you."

"You told me," I said encouragingly.

He finished the scotch and waved for another. "Well. No offense, Mack. But I hope you don't find his informant. Some rocks remain better unturned."

The bartender set another down.

"Too late, I'm afraid."

That stopped him. His refreshed glass paused halfway to his mouth.

"You did it?" he asked.

"I did it. Pretty sure."

"How sure?"

"Seventy-five percent."

"Huh." He set the glass down and stared into it. Hunched over the bar a bit.

"Haven't told Calvin yet."

"Huh."

"I asked one of Calvin's connections about what Calvin would do once he found the informant."

"And?"

"Chainsaws and an ax, is what I was told."

"Jesus Christ. What, like in *Scarface*?" he blurted.

"That's what I said. Great minds, you know?"

"Mack. Let's be serious for a minute. If Calvin kills the informant, you could be charged as an accomplice. Shit, I'd do the work pro bono. I'm not trying to be nasty but..."

"You're just flattering me," I said.

"I'm not saying the charges will stick. Up to a jury. But you'd at least be charged." His face had gone a little white. "Jesus. A chainsaw? Prissy old Summers?"

"I was told a much larger man would hold the handle."

"Shit," he said.

"It took me longer than I assumed. To find the informant."

He didn't respond.

I continued, "Because I'd been looking for a male."

He still didn't say anything. But he'd been kinda rocking with his weight leaning against the counter and he stopped.

"Just my natural masculine prejudices," I said. "You know?"

He took a drink. Turned his eyes to the television. Back down to the drink. Picked up his phone. Set it down again. The muscle in his jaw was flexing.

"Responsibility is a heavy thing," I said. "You're feeling it."

"Of course I am."

"Now you know what I'm feeling. They're going to kill her, Bill. With a chainsaw."

"A chainsaw," he repeated softly.

"And you won't be able to pin it on him."

"You told me you wouldn't reveal the informant's identity to Calvin," he said.

"I did say that."

"You told me you were doing this only to take the fucker's money. And to warn the informant that he or she had been found out."

"More or less," I said.

"Because you're one of the good guys."

"I even wear Superman boxers. But it's complicated. Like you said, he's better connected than I assumed."

"You were at this bar waiting for me," he realized. "Weren't you."

"Brad Thompson told me you come here."

"What do you want me to do? My hands are tied. I could lose my job. Lose my bar card. You don't need my help. Just go warn...the person you suspect."

"I'm going to. But I need some assurance I got the right person."

He twitched his shoulders. "I can't help you. Maybe just let the thing drop. Tell Summers you can't find the informant."

"Bill, it's taken me less than a month. It wasn't that hard. If I don't report, he'll find someone who will. Your informant is going to be found. Calvin's a man bent on revenge, a man with money and dangerous colleagues in his corner. It's only a matter of time."

"Jesus." He went back to staring into his drink.

"Tell me who it is."

"I can't."

"Then take a ride with me. We'll go warn her together. We'll figure something out."

He finished his second scotch. Tilted the glass up until the lone ice cube dropped into his mouth. Crunched it noisily. Waved for another. The bartender brought a new glass and took the old one away.

He said, "Chainsaws, huh."

"And an ax," I reminded him helpfully.

On screen the Cubs were congratulating each other on field. They'd beaten the Yankees 5-2.

He gulped half the glass and said, "I can't tell you a thing." He picked up his phone and ran his finger across the screen for sixty seconds and set it down without turning it off. He'd set it halfway between us. "What I'm going to do is go to the bathroom, Mack. Then I'm coming back to get my phone and go home. Because I'm not telling you a thing. You understand?"

"I understand."

He shoved away from the bar and walked toward the back. He moved like a man who'd consumed two and a half scotches in ten minutes.

It had to be Mrs. Hunt. Had to be. Bill hadn't argued with my implication that the informant was a woman.

I picked up his phone. He'd opened an email and left it on screen. The email had been sent months ago. I scanned.

I had to be right. My heart betrayed me and quickened slightly, the coward.

The email concerned the Calvin Summers case. I scrolled down. Kept reading.

Bingo.

There it was. In black and white.

The informant.

I set the phone back onto the polished bar and turned it off and finished my glass of gin.

Huh.

What do you know.

I was wrong.

25

It was after six o'clock. Probably too late to catch anyone in an office. But I knocked on Ronnie's heavy office door anyway. It was open.

Natasha Gordon, the receptionist, said, "Sorry sir, but the office... Oh. It's you."

"You could pretend to be excited. Beautiful people like myself have fragile egos," I said.

"I'll do better next time."

Natasha was closing up shop. She had dark circles under her eyes and much of her pretty brown hair had pulled loose from the...whatever it was that kept her hair up in the back. Her desk had been organized into neat piles and she was shrugging into a dark blue cardigan.

"Is Ronnie in?"

"Ms. Summers has gone home for the day. Can I take a message?"

"That's okay," I said. "I'm here to talk with you."

"With me," she said and a little color drained from her face.

"Mind if I sit?"

She didn't answer.

I sat.

"You found Mr. Summers's informant?" she asked.

"I have."

Natasha picked up her purse and set it in her lap and held it like a shield. "How?"

"I met Mrs. Hunt in Franklin Country. Boyd's wife. We talked."

"Oh?" she said.

"She hates me, though, which boggles the mind. I also met Alicia Gordon."

Natasha stayed quiet.

"I like Alicia. She's got spirit," I said.

She nodded.

I set my hand on the desk and twisted Natasha Gordon's name-plate around until it faced her instead of me. "I'm embarrassed it took me that long to connect the last names."

Natasha Gordon's hands went to her mouth and the rest of the color drained from her face.

"Alicia Gordon is your sister," I said.

"Yes."

"She is a prostitute."

"Yes. And she won't quit," Natasha said.

"Won't or can't. Some things aren't easy."

She nodded and refused to look away from my eyes. "We've talked to her. A hundred times. My mother and I, both. She's dating a worthless man. She has no future. No plans. She's stopped taking my calls."

"I see the resemblance between you two but it's faint."

"We have different fathers. Mine is still in Franklin County but hers is long gone."

"Gordon is your mother's last name."

"Yes," she said.

"You told me that you knew Mrs. Hunt from childhood. You grew up near her and she became a surrogate grandparent. Looked after you and Alicia?"

"We've always been close. Mrs. Hunt's youngest daughter was a few years older than me but we were friends and I played on the dairy farm."

"And then you grew up. No more innocent halcyon days. Got a

real job. But Alicia can't get her act together. Has no fatherly influence. She starts sleeping with guys for money and you can't make her stop and her mother can't make her stop and Mrs. Hunt can't make her stop."

"Alicia's boyfriend truly doesn't care, as long as she makes enough to keep cable television." She didn't speak with anger or frustration but rather with a resigned exhaustion. I'd heard that tone before, from families exasperated with loved ones. It was a lonely sound.

I continued, "Let me guess about the rest. One day you discover Alicia works the trailer parks owned by Calvin Summers. And that she isn't paid by the customers but rather by someone in charge. And you assume that someone is the owner."

"Of course. The bastard is into everything, from what I can tell."

"And you found yourself in a serendipitous situation. Because your sister's pimp, let's call him, is Calvin Summers — who is the father of your employer, and he's in this office consistently and he'd accidentally sent an email disclosing his illegal tax evasion."

Natasha had begun to cry. The muscles around her mouth quivered and her eyes reddened and moistened. Her breaths came in gasps. She looked tiny, as though her physical dimensions had shrunk.

"You're going to be okay, Natasha. I promise. I need to get the facts straight first. Okay?"

"Okay," she said, though she didn't believe me. She wiped at her nose with her sleeve.

"You examined the Calvin Summers financial email and spotted the tax evasion."

"It's my job to look through emails." She shrugged. "Of course I found it."

"And armed with this ammunition you spotted a possible salvation for your sister. You could put her pimp into jail. So you contacted a commonwealth attorney who put you in touch with Bill Osborne, a federal prosecutor, and you gave him the evidence. Right?"

"It didn't work. Mr. Summers went to jail and Alicia kept whoring herself."

"That's because you assumed Calvin was her pimp. But he's not. In fact, I don't think Calvin knows a thing about the prostitution."

Her face was blank. "What."

"Calvin Summers is very hands-off. He gives his underlings space to operate because he doesn't like to get his hands dirty. Within this margin, Wayne Cross initiated the prostitution side business. He sees himself as an up-and-comer, skimming off Calvin's marijuana plants and his moonshine stills, and he hired prostitutes without consulting his employer."

"I didn't know any of that."

"I know. I'm fitting the puzzle pieces together out loud for both our benefits," I said. "Point is, you sent the wrong man to jail. Even though Calvin deserved to be there."

"So what happens now? Mr. Summers will kill me. You're not going to tell him?"

"I have a responsibility to my client. I will do what I was hired to do and I will tell him you're the informant," I said. "And you need to be long gone by then."

"But..." The color in her face had gone past white. Now she looked gray. Or purple. Or green. All of it. "But...this is my whole life...what do...what will..."

"No matter what I do, you need to run. He'll find you sooner or later. Probably sooner, even without my help. Trust me. You didn't cover your tracks well enough."

"Run *where*?"

"Does Calvin keep any cash here? Perhaps inside the safe in Ronnie's office?"

A pause. Her hands stopped fidgeting with her purse. "He does."

"Do you know the combination?"

"I do. Ms. Summers gave it to me just last month."

"Steal it. All of it. Get in your car and go. Pick up Alicia and get out of here and don't stop until you get to the Florida Keys. Or to Coronado Beach in San Diego."

She was holding her breath. "And do what?"

"You and Alicia get a place to stay and you both wait tables at a restaurant on the beach. You enroll in college and become a para-legal. Should be easy for you after this job. Just an idea."

"Wow." She drew a shuddering breath. "Wow. Okay."

"This is happening fast, I know."

"He'll be mad. He'll come after us," she said.

"I'm going to give him someone else to be mad at."

"Who?"

"Me. Or Wayne Cross. Depends on how smart Wayne is. Calvin Summers will be so mad at one of us or maybe both that he'll forget you. He'll see you the same way he sees the federal prosecutor — an asshole he can't do anything about."

"Will Mr. Summers kill you?"

"Maybe. He might try."

"You'll do all this? For me?"

"For you and Alicia, yes. And for myself too. If it makes sense, I need to do right by me. I voluntarily stepped into this mess."

Natasha rose. Took a moment to steady herself. She went into Ronnie's office and I heard the heavy machinery of her safe followed by a dull thud. She returned, her purse overflowing with green.

"You sure this is a good idea?" she asked.

"It's the only idea. Or at least the only one I can think of on short notice. I think Wayne'll be busted by the Franklin County sheriff soon and you need to be long gone by then."

"So...I just...go?"

"Withdraw all the cash from your accounts. Pack as much as your car will hold. Go get Alicia. Don't tell her where you're going. Stuff your trunk with her things, if she has any. Fill your tank with gas. Don't stop until you're in North Carolina, and then only for coffee and gas. Don't use your cards. Don't tell your mom where you're going. She can move out with you once you're settled."

"I can do that."

"I know. You're the strong one in the family. And it's about to pay off."

"You can tell I'm the strong one?"

"That's obvious. Your sister thinks so too. But remember, you can't make people change. Alicia won't suddenly heal. We can only love people as best we can," I said.

"And hope."

"And pray."

"I see why Ms. Summers likes you so much," she said.

Yowza.

Was I a lesser mortal I'd have grown ten-feet tall. Ronnie liked me *so* much. But I stayed calm. "Well. Yeah."

She took a deep breath and said again, "I can do this."

"Bill Osborne is outside in his car. He approves of the plan. He wants a few words before you go and he's going to follow you until you're at the Virginia border, even if it takes all night. I don't think he trusts me."

She bent and kissed me on the cheek. A long kiss. And then another one, softer, on my temple.

"Thank you," she said.

"You're welcome. Before you go, I need a favor."

"Anything."

I SAT on Ronnie's couch for thirty minutes in the semi-dark. Thinking about Natasha and Ronnie and about Calvin Summers. I enjoyed the smell of her office. Because I enjoyed everything about her.

I was tempted to go through her personal things and see if she wrote my name in hearts over and over, but I decided against it. I was a professional after all.

Kristin Payne texted me.

>> hey stranger

>> dinner tonight?

>> following by second base at my place

>> lol

I texted back.

Can't tonight.

Dinner soon.

Free later this week?

Then I called Ronnie.

She answered on the second ring. "Hello Mackenzie."

"Hello Ronnie."

"Do I have a good phone voice? I can speak huskier, if it means you'll call more often."

I said, "Are you coming to your office tomorrow?"

"I am. Will you be there? If so I might wear a robe only."

I stayed quiet a long time. So did she. I even liked how silence sounded if it was her making it.

She said, "Mackenzie?"

"Yes Ronnie."

"What are you thinking about?"

"You."

"What about me."

I said, "That I'm lonely. But when I talk with you it's not so bad."

Another long hush.

When she finally spoke it began with a shudder. The flirt was gone, replaced with raw emotion. "I feel it too. I think about you. All day."

"Cancel your appointments tomorrow morning. Don't come in until after lunch."

"Why?"

"I need your office early."

"Mackenzie," she said. "You're making me nervous. Can I trust you?"

"Do you trust me?"

"Yes, I do."

"Good. I won't let you down."

"I know," she said. "I'll arrive at one."

"I'll be here. And I'll explain."

"Will you be wearing a robe only?"

"There's no robe invented yet to contain all my burly rough-hewn testosterone."

"Try anyway."

"See you tomorrow."

26

Almost home.

I turned off Grandin and I yawned so big that I almost missed Kristin Payne. She was parked two blocks from my house, her car situated to provide a clear view of my driveway. Car off. No lights. Just waiting.

"I think Kix might be right about her," I told myself and I pulled into a spot on the street and I got out.

Her eyes snapped onto me and she jumped in her seat. Busted! For a moment she panicked and thought about racing away but maturity won out. So instead she sat and stewed in her humiliation. I knocked on the passenger window and she unlocked the door and I climbed in.

"Having a stakeout?" I said. "You need the essentials. You need coffee and food, both sweet and salty, and most importantly you need a pee bottle."

"A pee bottle. That's disgusting, Mack." Her head was propped on her elbow, which rested on the door. Her eyes were buried into her palm.

"Gonna pee on the neighbor's bushes instead? That's not disgusting?"

"I'm really embarrassed," she said.

"As you should be, you scamp, spying on me."

We were talking in the dark. Me looking at her, and her eyes closed. Our voices were compacted in the tiny space.

"It's just you never call me. And I texted you and you said you were busy, and I thought...I don't know what I thought."

"You thought you'd do what I do for a living," I said. "You wanted to gather more information before jumping to conclusions."

"When you put it that way, I sound less pathetic."

"That was not my intention."

Finally she glanced my way. "Look how big you are. I can't even see the seat. And your hair brushes the roof."

"I'm swollen with goodwill. Having a good day."

"At least one of us is," she said. "I fucked up."

"Perhaps your romantic notions aren't as casual as you intimated, even to yourself."

"I think you're right about the sex. It got a lot less casual after that. I'm a worldly modern girl with an advanced education. Surely, I thought, I can fuck who I want and not think twice. What am I, after all, other than an intelligent mammal? If dogs can screw whoever they want then I can too."

"Casual sex is a popular theory, espoused by savvy marketers and television writers. Seems to me that theory is only good for selling something. But again, this is based on anecdotal evidence. Not on objective facts."

"Okay, so whatever, fuck it, I like you. Not casually."

"Great. Let's get dinner later this week," I said.

"You're not put off by my jealous and possessive behavior?"

"It doesn't speak well for our future. But who knows."

"You're keeping me around to get your mind off the other girl," she said. "Right?"

"Maybe. I don't want to lie to you about that."

"It's jarring being with a man who is so honest. Even when the honesty hurts," she said.

"I don't know how else to be."

"You weren't with that girl tonight?"

"I was not. She and I are not dating."

"Are you dating anyone other than me?" she asked.

"No."

"Then what's my problem?"

"I don't know. You're too nosey, maybe?"

"Mack, can you do me a favor? Go home and pretend this didn't happen. I'm going back to my place and sticking my head in the freezer."

"Sure." I got out and closed the door and gave her a wave. She started the car and drove off, gravel spitting under her tires.

It was best, I decided, if Kix didn't hear about this.

27

I listened to Manny snore on my floor until 1:15am while I tossed fitfully. When I woke at 5:30am he was still going strong, the jerk.

I made coffee and eggs and bacon, and I got Kix out of bed when he called an hour and a half later. He ate dry cereal and pieces of a pear, and he rejected a bite of my eggs. He liked to eat with one hand and hold mine with his other. I did not discourage this arrangement.

"Nana peas," he said, which meant, "Give me bananas this instant."

"We don't have any," I told him. "Sorry kid."

He shrugged and drank his milk.

Manny came down, yawning and scratching his stubble, which was sparse. The man was mostly hairless.

"Breakfast in the pan," I said. "You should reheat it."

"Don't be bossy, señor."

"Guess who Calvin Summer's informant is," I said. "You'll never get it."

"Ronnie's secretary."

"What the hell."

"Remember, I staked that place out for you in the fall. Told you about the secretary. She too cute and perfect to be innocent."

"You could have told me this ironclad reasoning weeks ago."

He got coffee and cold eggs and salsa, and he sat down. "You get lazy. What will you do?"

"She's long gone. Halfway to paradise by now. Later this morning I plan on getting beat up by Wayne."

"Want some Hispanic reinforcement?"

"No. Got myself into this mess. I'll get myself out of it."

"You just want Ronnie think you're tough."

"Agreed."

It was after 8:00am. I went into the other room and called Calvin.

He answered and said, "This better be good, August. I'm next up on the tee box."

"Golfing? But it's chilly."

"What do you want."

"I got your informant."

"Holy shit. Okay, hold on a second." In the background I heard him making an excuse and then the rattle of a motor. Pulling his golf cart out of line. "I'm ready."

"It's Ronnie's receptionist."

"Ronnie's receptionist? What's her name, Natalie? You sure?"

"Natasha. Meet me there in an hour. Ronnie's out of the office today," I said.

"Jesus. My fucking attorney's receptionist."

"Ronnie didn't tell her. It was your email. Meet me in an hour."

"I'll be there. What are you going to do?"

"Nothing. I'm not a mob hit man," I said.

"Then how do I handle this?"

"Bring Wayne."

"What am I paying you for?"

"To find your informant. Which I've done. I'll explain how, when you arrive."

"Fine." He hung up.

I went back into the kitchen.

"But the informant is already gone," Manny noted.

"Indeed."

"He gonna be angry, amigo."

"I have that effect," I said. "But at least he'll be angry at me. Or at Wayne. Not at Natasha and not at Ronnie."

"You not going to last in organized crime. Too soft."

"Who says I want to be in organized crime?" I asked.

"Maybe best don't take their *dinero* in the future."

"I only took it because his daughter smiled at me. Does that help?"

"Ask him and see. What will you do?" he asked.

"Sometimes, when there are no good options, it's best to absorb the punishment instead of dishing it out."

"Estupido."

"She's worth it," I said.

"Who? Ronnie or the receptionist?"

"Both."

WAYNE ARRIVED FIRST. He sat in his monster truck with a camouflage ball cap and sunglasses on, staring straight ahead. Ten minutes later Calvin Summers pulled into the parking lot in his silver Lexus. My shiny Honda lost a bit of its sheen by comparison.

All three of us exited our vehicles at the same time.

Like in a movie about tough guys.

"The secretary in there?" Calvin said.

"Haven't checked. Ronnie said she should be."

"Where's Veronica?" he asked.

"Out on business."

Wayne coughed out a plug of tobacco. He spat a few times and said, "Told you I wasn't the informant, motherfucker."

I held up my hands — oops, silly me.

Calvin said, "We're going in. The three of us will put her into the back of my car and Wayne will ride with me." He was nervous. Didn't like it. Plus he was doing it wrong. This should be done at night, not during the day in the city. "Let's go," he said.

Ronnie's office was on the second floor. We marched up and found the door unlocked. Calvin looked at us for reassurance and he pushed into the office.

It was, of course, empty.

Calvin went into Ronnie's office and came out. "Where is she?"

Wayne checked the bathroom and conference room. No Natasha. I watched from the door.

A frustrated Calvin went behind Natasha's desk and kicked at the swivel chair. "Fucking waste of time." He glared at her desk and at the stacks of papers, hands on hips.

"She ain't here," Wayne said. He scoffed at me. "Thanks for the brilliant idea."

Calvin's gaze dropped to Natasha's keyboard. And the note on top. He picked it up and read it. Then read it again. "What the hell."

Wayne said, "What? What is it?"

"Is this a joke? Is this even her handwriting?" Calvin picked up Natasha's notepad to compare the script. "This is her handwriting."

"What's it say?" Wayne asked.

Calvin was turning a shade of crimson. Staring at the note.

"Summers," Wayne said. "What is it?"

He spoke slowly. "This is a note from the receptionist. She admits she passed the fucking email to the government."

Wayne made a whistling sound.

"And that she's fled the country," Summers continued.

Wayne and I both grunted.

"Girl knows what's good for her," Wayne said.

"She also says you're stealing from me, Wayne," Calvin said.

"Bullshit."

"She says so. Right here. Why would she say that, Wayne?"

"Lemme see the note," Wayne said, reaching for the paper.

Summers pulled it out of his reach. We all stood in close proximity. The reception area had grown smaller with three grown men around the desk.

"This true, Wayne?" Summers asked.

"Of course not."

I cleared my throat and said, "I humbly disagree."

Calvin's eyes shifted to me. There was the hint of a dangerous man underneath. That he was more than a simple rich white guy. "Talk, August."

"August don't know shit," Wayne said.

"Wayne has a side business he hasn't told you about," I said. "I confirmed it two days ago. And that's the reason your informant has fled."

Wayne had gone still. He towered over Calvin. Had I not been there, this would be the point when Wayne beat him to death.

"Side business? What side business?" Calvin asked.

"Prostitution."

"Prostitution? The fuck. So you're a pimp?"

"Not a pimp," Wayne said. "I run girls around the county. Don't mean I steal. Proves nothing."

"What's this got to do with me?" Calvin asked. "I don't care if Wayne's selling girls."

"Two things," I said. "I got two people saying Wayne steals from everyone. Including you, because you're too hands-off."

"Fuck you, I don't steal."

"You've got a safe full of cash in your basement says otherwise."

"My basement?" Wayne trembled with anger. This was the tricky part. If Wayne was smart he'd play it cool, act like that was legitimate profit.

"Wayne?" Summers asked. "What cash?"

"You fucking went into my basement."

"I took pictures too," I said helpfully. "Also you need a dehumidifier down there. I worry about black mold."

"You're a dead man, August."

"Nuh-uh. I don't have black mold."

"Wayne, this true?" Summers said. "What the fuck."

"He's right, Wayne. Black mold is not something you want to ignore."

Calvin said, "August, shut up with the mold. So Wayne's stealing. He's got a safe full of my cash in his basement. After all I've done for him."

"He's skimming off the marijuana and moonshine profits," I said.

Wayne glared murder at me. It was daunting. I was terribly daunted.

Scummy guy like him should have denied it, but he was too stupid. He thought he'd been caught red-handed but in reality I had no proof. So he stayed quiet and admitted his guilt.

"What's the other thing?" Summers asked. "You said there were two things."

"The other thing is your informant. Wayne had the brilliant idea to hire Natasha Gordon's sister."

"Who's Natasha Gordon?"

I picked up the nameplate. "Ronnie's receptionist. Wayne hired her sister."

"What, as a hooker?"

"Yes. Alicia Gordon. That's how I discovered Natasha was your informant. Natasha got your incriminating email and she examined it. She also thought you were her sister's pimp because Alicia worked at your trailer parks. She couldn't get her sister to quit, so she thought maybe if you went to jail then the business would dry up and Alicia would come clean. Little did she know that Wayne was the pimp and not you."

"So I went to jail," Calvin said, "because Wayne is a pimp."

"To be fair, the tax evasion didn't help."

Wayne hit me. Give him credit, the man hit quick. And his fists were the size of bowling balls. I was ready for it and he still landed.

I rocked backwards into the wall, chimes going off.

He fished for his gun. Idiot had it hidden under his long checkered shirt.

Even dazed I got mine out first. Thumbed off the safety with a sexy click.

"Damn it, Wayne," I said. He held up his hands. Couldn't get his gun in time. "That's twice you got me. This face pays the bills."

"Put away your gun and hit me back, motherfucker."

"I'm going to."

"Yeah?"

"Yeah. Draw your gun with two fingers and set it on the table. If you use three fingers I'll shoot you in the shoulder just like I shot your boy Parks."

Summers said, "Parks?"

"Wayne sent some guys to kill me. He got worried I was near the truth."

"What happened?"

"I discouraged them," I said.

"And shot one of them in the shoulder?"

"Parks was quite discouraged," I said.

"So now what? You two idiots hit each other, find out who's the toughest?"

"Essentially."

"Why?"

"We're sophisticated gentlemen," I said, wincing against the pain gathering in my cheekbone.

"August, sometimes I wish you'd cut the bullshit and give a straight answer," Summers said.

"Wayne's sucker punched me twice. I told him not to do it again. Now he learns a hard lesson."

"What if he wins?" Calvin asked.

"Then we're both in trouble."

Wayne set his .45 on Natasha's desk, using two fingers as directed. "Good?"

"Good," I said.

I hit him with my left hand, the hand not holding my gun. A short pop under his eye. He staggered back and I slipped my gun into its holster.

My blood pumped hot and my focus winnowed down to his hands and face.

Calvin picked up Wayne's gun and held it awkwardly, like holding a fish.

Wayne swung at me and I caught it on the back of my left arm and I hit him again. A straight right that caught him in the nose and he bled immediately. I tried for a left hook but he bulldozed through, picked me up around the waist and dropped me hard onto Natasha's desk. Calvin jumped into the corner and the desk splintered and broke and both of us fell through. The computer monitor landed hard beside my head. I lay on my back and he on top and I hit him again and again, hammer strokes from each side into his ears and cheekbones. He roared and raised up and clenched his fists together and brought them down simultaneously. Wayne had never fought MMA before, didn't know how to wrestle on the floor. I took the blow on my shoulder and it didn't hurt like he intended. I kneed him in the groin. Then I doubled the same knee up and kicked him off. He fell back and groaned and rolled in pain. The room had gotten smaller and hotter.

I got to my feet, breathing heavy. Some of the fight had gone out from him. Both his ears and cheeks were bleeding and so was his nose. He tried to rush me again. More of a drunken fall. I kneed him in the face and brought around a right hook. A solid connection that nearly broke my knuckles. He fell into his face. Tried to get up but couldn't.

"Now we understand each other, Wayne," I said between pants, echoing his words from that day at the moonshine still. "That's how it's gonna be."

Calvin held out Wayne's pistol. "Here. Kill the bastard with his own gun."

"I'm not a hit man, Summers."

"You work for me, damn it."

"Used to. You hired me to find out who sent you to jail. Case closed. It was Natasha and Alicia and Wayne. Now we're done. You want him dead you'll have to get your hands dirty this time."

"I'm not killing him. How much for you to do it? Kill him and dispose of the corpse. Name your price."

"I won't kill him for you. I didn't even beat him up for you. That was for me."

"What do we do with him?" he asked.

Wayne groaned something from the thin carpet.

"We don't do anything. I was you, I'd let him go. Call Marcus Morgan, see what he advises."

"Good idea. Yeah, I'll call Marcus."

"You hear that, Wayne?" I called. "Local mafioso is going to hear about you. If you're smart you'll get in your truck and find a different county to ruin. Not Floyd, because Clay Fleming doesn't like you."

Wayne made a miserable sound. He was able to get to his feet but he wouldn't look at us. His shirt had begun to absorb blood. He glanced sullenly at the pistol in Calvin's hand and he lumbered out of the office and down the stairs.

"Good help is hard to find, eh August? Damn, you knocked the shit out of him. Never thought I'd see that."

"I'd keep track of Wayne. If he doesn't vacate town then you should hire a guy to walk around with you for a while. Someone like Fat Susie to discourage all evildoers. Also, one final professional advisement — if you want good help, promote Scott to Wayne's abandoned position. Scott from Happy Fields. He's loyal to you and hard working and he deserves it."

"Is that so? Loyal to me? Consider it done."

"Good."

"I still owe you money," Calvin said. "I'm good for it."

"I know."

"You did good, August."

"I know this. But our working relationship is over. I won't work for the mob again," I said.

"The mob? Don't be so dramatic. I'm a businessman, same as you, same as Marcus. Besides, who pays as much as us? Nobody, that's who."

"I'm getting some ice from Ronnie's office. Goodbye Summers," I said.

"Come on now. Let's end on friendly terms. This is a handshake world we live in."

"No. My hand hurts."

"Ahh, who needs you. I'm going to golf," he said.

"Wear a glove. Gotta keep those hands clean."

28

I woke on Ronnie's couch. The bag of ice had melted and lay on the floor. An angel perched on the side of the couch and she kissed me on the mouth. Not nearly long enough.

"Hello Mackenzie," she said.

"Hello Ronnie."

Her lips curved in a smile and she pushed a strand of hair off my forehead. "You've destroyed my desk."

"Natasha's desk. Her name was on it."

"You've also hurt your face. There is a giant swollen bruise. Shall I make it better?"

"If you insist."

She kissed me again. Our lips touched and she took a deep breath and held it. We pressed into each other. I counted heartbeats. I allowed myself ten before pulling away.

She said, "I wish you were always on this couch when I arrived."

"You knew," I said. "You knew Natasha was your father's informant."

"I knew nothing for certain."

"You suspected."

"An indistinct suspicion," she said. "In other words, I'm not surprised to learn the truth. Is she safe?"

"She is. She stole your father's cash and collected her sister, and hopefully they're sitting on a beach and enjoying a new freedom by now."

She smiled and nodded, a satisfied expression. "Perfect. I hope so too. How much cash?"

"I'm not sure. All of it?"

"Wow. He'll be displeased."

"Good," I said. "Let me guess. You couldn't bring yourself to directly betray your father. If you knew for certain about Natasha then you'd face choices you couldn't stand. Right?"

"Yes Mackenzie."

"So you hired me because you were worried she'd get caught. You knew I'd find the informant and if it was Natasha then I'd do the right thing."

"Yes Mackenzie."

"What a smart girl you are."

"Not that smart," she said. "But I trusted the right man."

"I am the right man."

She unbuttoned the top three buttons of my shirt and laid her hand flat on my chest. "Yes. You are."

"I told him I wouldn't work for him again. It's too complicated."

"Yes. It's very complicated. Did he hit you?"

"No. That's insulting. Wayne hit me," I said.

"Why?"

"Wayne was stealing from him. I conveyed this information, along with the Natasha revelation. Wayne didn't appreciate being exposed."

"What happened to Wayne?" she asked.

"He looks much worse than me. I disciplined him and let him leave. I expect he'll head further south soon. Your father is well connected."

"You disciplined him."

"Yes."

"That's kind of sexy."

"Doesn't feel sexy," I said. "Feels like I broke that hardwood desk with my back."

"Take off your shirt. I'll give you a massage. And while you're at it you can lose the pants."

"You are a vixen."

"Does that mean no?" she asked.

"Not while you're engaged."

"I wish you'd stop bringing that up. It makes me sad."

"I know the feeling." I took her hand and kissed it.

"Look how big you are. This isn't a small couch. But I'm not convinced it's big enough for both of us to...wrestle on."

If I stayed there much longer my defenses would come crashing down and our complex relationship would go absolutely nuclear. I stood and picked up the ice bag and threw it away.

"You need a new desk," I said.

"And a new receptionist to sit behind it. Can I hire you?"

"You strike me as the kind of boss who would molest me."

"Daily. But you'd enjoy it," she said.

"I would. You wouldn't even need to pay me a salary."

"If you won't be my receptionist then I'll find more cases which require a handsome private detective."

We stayed still, watching each other.

"I need to go," I said.

"I know."

"I'm going."

Neither of us moved. It felt like invisible cords had wrapped around us, binding me to her. I couldn't decide whether to hold my breath or gasp for air.

She smiled. That big curvy smile which shook my foundations.

"Why the smile?" I asked.

"Because. You love me."

"That's a big word to throw around. Are you sure?"

"I have an indistinct suspicion. But my instincts are often correct," she said. "You love me. And it's the only good thing in my life."

"You're a hot mess."

"I know this."

"Goodbye Ronnie," I said.

"Goodbye Mackenzie. I'll see you soon."

29

I sat in my office, scanning potential assignments via email. As usual, children were missing. Spouses were cheating. Statements required taking. Superman was needed.

And I, Clark Kent.

A woman walked into my office. She was so short and slight that she hadn't triggered the groaning stairs. I stood and said, "Hello, Mrs. Hunt."

"Mr. August." Unless my eyes deceived me, she was wearing the same dress as that day in the Dairy Queen parking lot. Her hands were clasped together in front. Strong hands, accustomed to hard work. "I come to Roanoke to speak with Mr. Summers's accountant, Tom Bradshaw. I meet with the man once a quarter."

"Nice guy. Very loyal. Got his ducks in a row. Please have a seat."

"No, I won't. I will not stay. I only came to apologize. Seems I had you wrong," she said.

"No one ever apologizes to me. Can I record this?"

"Don't be an ass, Mr. August."

"Tall order. Ass is my modus operandi," I said.

"Alicia is gone."

"Her sister Natasha took her. They've got some money and they are starting a new life."

She nodded curtly. "Thank you," she said. "Those girls are precious to me."

"You're welcome. But I did it for me."

"I don't follow."

"What am I, if I'm not helping a girl get out of prostitution? If I'm not helping Natasha escape a violent man? I'd be a coward. A simple functionary. Couldn't live with myself," I said. "I did it to define what I am and what I am not."

"I had been looking at you wrong, Mr. August."

"Maybe you weren't. I was making a mess. But we got lucky and it turned out. The chips fell into a pattern which benefitted us," I said.

"I won't pretend to know what that means and I don't care to. I owed you an apology and there it is. I'll be off."

"Please give my regards to your husband. He's a man I admire."

"I believe the feeling will be mutual," she said, pausing at the door, "once I tell him about the girls."

"Aw shucks."

"The foolish old man is talking about taking our savings and moving to the beach. Closer to the children."

"You must. A no-brainer," I said.

"Well, truth be told, I'd be glad to be rid of that Calvin Summers."

"Yes, a sentiment we share."

"You won't keep working for him?" she asked.

"Doubtful. But it's complicated. I'm twitterpated with his daughter."

She frowned, like she wished she'd departed thirty seconds ago. "Well. Nothing good will come from that, I'm sure. That girl's got secrets."

She left.

"I know this," I told myself. With a fair amount of trepidation. "But she's worth it."

The End

Dear Reader,

I hope you enjoyed Book Two, *The Second Secret*. (You did)
I have three suggestions for your next novel.

One) The Desecration of All Saints. It's a stand-alone Mackenzie mystery, not part of the series cannon. Mackenzie is hired to investigate a priest. It takes place directly before the novel you just finished.

Two) Book Three of the series, Flawed Players. A sneak peek is included below.

Three) If you like, I'll email you The Last Teacher, Mackenzie's prequel.

To simplify, here is my recommended reading order:

1) August Origins (Book One)
2) Desecration of All Saints (Book One and a Half)
3) The Second Secret (Book Two)
4) Flawed Players (Book Three)
5) Last Teacher (Prequel - I'll email you the book for free)
6) Aces Full (Book Four)
7) Only the Details (Book Five)
8) Ghost in Paradise (Short Story. I'll email you.)
9) Good Girl (Book Six)
10) The Supremacy License (Manny/Sinatra, Book One)
11) Wild Card (Manny/Sinatra, Book Two)

Desecration and *Last Teacher* don't necessarily have to be read in order.
Nor do the Manny/Sinatra books.
Clearly a great adventure awaits you. It's going to be a great month.

SNEAK PEEK

A preview of the beginning of chapter one, *Flawed Players*, Mackenzie August book three.

PRIVATE DETECTIVES—AN unsavory group, most times. Gumshoes are usually ex-cop or ex-military, and the *ex-* is for a reason. Like for being an ass.

I collaborated with local gumshoes on occasion. Fat, lazy, unshaven, unscrupulous, and broke. Teeth weren't great either. Bottom-feeders giving the rest a bad name, often extorting their clients once an investigation yielded dirt.

It was this reputation that prompted me to set out potpourri, a masculine scent purchased online. Only us noble-hearted stalwarts, stuffed with scruples, would set out potpourri. Made me think of sawdust, gun oil, and...Glenlivet 21, maybe. I was contemplating the exact recipe when the wooden stairs outside my office popped and creaked.

In walked a man. Handsome guy. Takes one to recognize one. Blonde hair, trim, great cheekbones. Looked like he rowed crew at

Harvard. His jeans were professionally distressed and his white button-up was cuffed at the sleeves. I knew Allen Edmonds when I saw them.

I sucked in my gut.

Then I noticed his socks didn't match. So I probably didn't need to show off.

"Do you know who I am?" he asked.

"Robert Redford's stunt double?"

He pursed his lips. "You haven't seen me in the newspaper."

"Be serious. No one reads the newspaper."

"Thank god. I'm relieved you haven't." He dropped into my client chair as though just finishing a marathon. "Paranoia, I suppose."

I gave him a moment to recompose. Looked like he needed it—he was sweating.

He said, "Feels like I've been stamped with a scarlet letter, walking here. I can't believe I'm in a private detective's office."

"It's good, right?"

"It's not black and white. In the movies, they're always…"

"Sam Spade, Philip Marlowe," I offered. "Mike Hammer."

"Right. My father, he enjoyed those."

"Would it help if I drank scotch? I'm willing."

"I've been charged with something I didn't do."

"Ah," I said.

"And the police show a disinclination to pursue any other suspect. I retain absolutely no faith in the justice system, after this debacle."

"Understandable. The only justice in this world is the justice you take."

His eyes, a handsome brown, narrowed. "Who are you quoting?"

"Don't remember. Someone brilliant."

"Can you help?"

I said, "I can. But the more germane question is, do I want to?"

"Why would you not? Is this not your livelihood? You're an investigator for hire, yes?"

"For a mercenary, my tastes are discriminating." I hoped by now he'd noticed my good potpourri.

"Well, good for you, I suppose," he said. "I didn't realize your profession afforded such luxuries. It appears you've been hit recently."

"You're on thin ice, sir."

He pointed to my eye. "Contusion along your orbicularis oculi. Can't imagine someone attacking you and getting away with it. You're big."

"I let him. For the sake of my tough guy image. What is that which the police purports you did?"

The air seemed to go out of him. He leaned forward, rested his elbows on his knees, dropped his head. "I live on Tradd Street. Do you know it?"

"I do."

"What do you know?"

I crossed my ankles and laced my fingers over my stomach. My flat stomach, despite what Kix said. "Tradd Street is home to Roanoke denizens believing themselves to be cream of the crop. Royalty. Lots of money. Near Cornwallis."

"Well said. They stylize themselves as upper crust. We, I guess. We pay a mint for the nomenclature. The name Tradd has value built in. It's funny, isn't it, how value develops organically from social hierarchies."

"Or perhaps not so organically."

He asked, "What do you mean?"

"There's nothing natural about, say, botox."

"Or surgical enhancements. Of course, you're correct. It's not organic at all."

"I'm not judging. I could be classified as a fan of certain enhancements," I said.

"Perhaps I should have worded it—it's sick how we manufacture value by building our own pedestals, and then pretending the pedestals appeared organically."

"Tradd by any other name…. Has it worked?

"Has what?"

"Has the street satisfied the great gaping hole in your heart? As

Thoreau said, do you no longer lead a life of quiet desperation?" I asked. Only top tier detectives quote Thoreau. I should get that on my door. Sam Spade never quoted the greats. Spenser, on the other hand...

He said, "No, but...there's a certain gratification in reaching the pinnacle. Yet it's a hollow victory. We're the dogs who caught the car and it turns out the car isn't as advertised."

"The dogs who caught the car. I enjoy that analogy. I'm going to use it in the future without giving you credit. But we've waded into deep waters. Pray, continue with your story."

He nodded.

"As I was saying. I live on Tradd. We suffered a recent rash of burglaries. The burglars defeated the alarm systems and flummoxed police investigators. The street is indignant and atwitter."

"What has been stolen?"

"Art. Collectors items. Smallish treasures which could be sold easily, valued in the tens of thousands."

"Smallish treasure worth ten thousand. Was it a baseball signed by Babe Ruth?"

He didn't seem to hear. "It was for this crime that I was charged last week."

"Heavens. Did you do it?"

...

READ the rest of Mackenzie's next adventure, an investigation into the sordid underbelly of Roanoke's royalty. Click here for Flawed Players